LINGERING SHADOWS

When Stephanie Nelson settled in San Francisco, she hoped to leave her tragic past behind her. Although she had been proven innocent of the murder of her husband, Stephanie feared the effect the scandal would have on her new job, her new friends, and especially her new love — a handsome young architect. And those fears were realized when a figure from her past appeared, threatening not only scandal for Stephanie, but her life as well!

LINGERING SHADOWS

When Stephanie Nelson settled in San Francisco, she hoped to leave her tragic past behind her. Although she had been proven innocent of the murder of her husband, Stephanie found the effect the scandal would have on her new job, her new friends, and especially her new love — handsome young architect... And those fears were realized when a figure from her past appeared, threatening not only Stephanie's job but her life as well.

NANCY MacDOUGALL KENNEDY

◆

LINGERING SHADOWS

Complete and Unabridged

LINFORD
Leicester

First published in the
United States of America

First Linford Edition
published September 1995

British Library CIP Data

Kennedy, Nancy MacDougall
  Lingering shadows.—Large print ed.—
  Linford romance library
  I. Title II. Series
  823.914 [F]

  ISBN 0–7089–7774–X

Published by
F. A. Thorpe (Publishing) Ltd.
Anstey, Leicestershire
Set by Words & Graphics Ltd.
Anstey, Leicestershire
Printed and bound in Great Britain by
T. J. Press (Padstow) Ltd., Padstow, Cornwall

This book is printed on acid-free paper

1

IT was not that he was a difficult man to work for, Stephanie Nelson reflected as she sat erect, pencil in hand, waiting for him to stop woolgathering and get on with the dictation. But he had some exasperating faults, most notably his moods of whimsy, one of which seemed to engage him now.

She had worked for the architectural firm of Bayliss & MacArthur, Inc., for just three weeks, but already she preferred Paul Bayliss to his unpredictable partner.

Stifling a sigh, Stephanie recrossed her legs, hoping the movement would distract him enough to get this letter finished. When it did not, she tried frowning at him. Really, she thought angrily, there was something so undignified, almost indecent, about

1

the way he was lying back in his swivel chair, feet on the desk and ankles crossed, his lazy face turned up to the high ceiling.

It *was* a lazy face, she decided. Everything about him was lazy. She wished fervently for the nerve to tell him to get with it!

"Where was I?" He untangled his long legs from the desk top, but continued to lie back in his chair, his big mouth forming a grin for his erect, and demure-looking secretary. "It can't be springtime in January, can it?" he queried. "Even you, honey, look a little sleepy."

He called all the girls honey, so the endearment could be ignored. Stephanie did not smile at his remark; she merely directed her frown downward to her notebook. "You've almost finished this letter, Mr. MacArthur," she said. "I could get it out for you tonight, if you would."

His absurdly long-lashed, sleepy blue eyes regarded her with mischief. "Would

2

the sky fall if we just skipped it altogether, Mrs. Nelson?"

"You said something about wanting to get it out tonight."

"Did I? Well, you see, honey, it's my tender heart that impedes the sternness of my mind. I hate to say no, don't you?"

She took refuge in silence, affecting interest in her notes, then with a thrust of stubbornness she said without looking up, "I should like to get this letter finished."

"Well, okay, finish it," he grinned. "You say no, honey, and make it sound as if we're doing them a favor."

She stood, inwardly pleased to be trusted to finish the letter, but unsmiling in case he was laughing at her. "I'll have it ready for your signature before you leave."

He let her reach the door before he called her and waited until she turned. "Don't you know what day this is? Didn't anyone tell you?"

She frowned, and with an edge of

3

sarcasm she repeated the day, month, and year.

"Good for you," he said. "Now, what else?"

"I can't think of anything offhand, Mr. MacArthur."

"I'm hurt." He pulled down his lips in imitation of misery. "I'm deeply hurt that you didn't notice, that no one told you, not even our know-it-all Ginny of the switchboard." He sat forward, shaking a finger at her. "I'll have you know, young lady, this is no ordinary day. This is the birthday of Alexander Dumas MacArthur!"

She killed the impulse to laugh by biting her lips. Alexander *Dumas*, she thought wildly. Oh, really, he was the most ridiculous, the most impossible —

"Don't laugh," he was cautioning. "My mother had a strong affinity for *La Dame aux Camélias* — that's Camille, you know. Mother still makes a point of explaining that I was named for the younger Dumas, not the elder. The elder wrote *The Count of Monte*

Cristo, but Mother never had any time for him. My mother is still a very romantic girl, despite age and a damnable wheelchair."

"Well, happy birthday, Mr. Mac-Arthur," she said helplessly. "Sorry I didn't know."

"You are? What would you have done, honey, sent me a card?" He shuffled a pile of such on his desk. "Baked me a cake? Bought me a present? Just what, Stephanie Nelson?"

"You like to tease, Mr. MacArthur."

"You like to tease, Mr. MacArthur," he mimicked, and again he pointed at her. "I know what I want from you for my birthday," he declared. "I want you, as of now, to cut out the *mister* bit!"

She thought of quiet, gentlemanly Mr. Bayliss with longing, and heartily wished this job did not entail secretarial service to both partners.

"Aw, go ahead," this partner was urging. "Try it. Say it loud and clear, and I'll call you Stephanie — no, I'll call you Steph, that has more zing to it. Now, go ahead, honey, say it.'Happy birthday, dear Mac!'"

"Happy birthday, Mac," she said through her teeth, and fled.

Alexander Dumas MacArthur lay back in his chair once more and grinned, then looked somewhat abashed. He supposed he had given her a hard time, but humorless women always raised the Old Nick in him. And this new secretary Paul had hired was a dilly.

Mrs. Stephanie Nelson, he mulled. He could not remember the husband's name. He sure didn't envy him. Mac thumped his chair as he sat forward suddenly. Holy Toledo, now he remembered — she was a widow. He grimaced, nonetheless. A less likely looking widow he had never seen. She looked more like his spinster cousin, Agatha, the music teacher.

Mac felt a little ashamed of having teased the new secretary, but just a little. She could, he decided, become

6

a big pain in the neck, with her stern mouth and cold eyes. Their last secretary had been sixty-five and a jolly old girl.

And it *was* his birthday. She had to have seen the cards in the mail, and he couldn't imagine little Ginny Goodwin not spreading the news. She must have *heard* Liz Peterson yell out, "Happy Birthday, dear Mac!"

Anyway, he grumbled, he just happened to think birthdays were fun. It was, of course, his mother's fault with her incurable sentimentality. She had planted deep the seeds of birthday joy when he was very young, saying a birthday was a person's own very special day.

Mac grinned. He could remember as a child believing utterly that the whole world stood quite still for a moment in silent tribute to the fact of his birth.

He stood at the window, looking down at the milling crowds, hurrying, amid the endless city noises. It all seemed sad. There seemed to be so little fun in people nowadays, so little time for just doing nothing, just realizing one's self.

He laughed deep in his throat as he turned back to his desk. He knew quite well that he was a sentimental slob and a born optimist, both traits inherited from his frail, lovely little mother, just as his sister, Beth, had inherited her beauty and their father's common sense. He, Mac, *looked* like his lawyer father, whose death two years before had left his mother looking her age for the first time, but in nature he was his mother all over again. And he was glad.

He stood, stretched, yawned. There was no way he could avoid the birthday party at his mother's house tonight, and part of him did not want to, but it meant appeasing lovely Tina Marshall, who was miffed at not being included in the party. Mac knew all too well that to bring a girl with him to his mother's house was tantamount to a marriage proposal.

His grin reappeared. Tina was a terrific woman, he conceded, but just a little slow at understanding he was not the marrying kind. His own father had not married until he was over forty. And I, chortled Mac, am still my father's son.

He sat down as Stephanie came in and laid the finished work on his desk, then stood back, her face expressionless. An unusual ripple of irritation touched Mac, and to hide it he scrawled his signature without reading the letter and pushed it toward her.

"Paul still here?" he asked, more sharply than he meant.

"Mr. Bayliss just left," she said, gathering up the unremarked work which she was proud of, and she could not help adding: "It *is* ten minutes to five."

"Okay, that's all." On his feet again, he shook himself into his topcoat, reached for his hat, and made for the door. "Good night, *Mrs.* Nelson," he growled.

Stephanie followed him out feeling rather amused. She supposed he was regretting his silliness. A grown man making all that fuss about his birthday, she had decided, was a definite sign of immaturity. Anyway, she shrugged, she preferred him gruff, as he had been in leaving, rather than silly.

She felt curiously depressed as she sat at her desk, folding the perfectly typed letter and sliding it into its envelope. Her job was very important to her. She felt that Mr. Bayliss liked her and approved her work, but Mr. MacArthur was doubtful, although he had voiced no complaints about her work.

She supposed she would have to practice laughing at his jokes. He was very popular with the other employees of the small company. And it seemed particularly small to Stephanie after her job back East. She whipped her mind away from the past. The present must be all that mattered.

She needed to feel secure in this job,

for she had no reserve funds, and with rent to pay, food to buy . . . At least, her clothes would do all right until spring.

Had she said good night to Mr. MacArthur? The thought made her uneasy. To comfort herself, she glanced about her office; she had never had an office of her own before.

It was large and well appointed. On either side were doors, leading to Mr. Bayliss' and Mr. MacArthur's offices. In front of her to the left a door led into the reception room down a wide hallway, and next to it a door led into Engineering, as it was called, where half a dozen young architects were lorded over by their girl Friday, one Liz Peterson.

Liz had been friendly, Stephanie thought warmly, which was important since they were the only two women in this wing, and the young architects were very polite. She sighed. She was aware that her air of quiet efficiency and studied aloofness put people off, but it seemed necessary to her survival. She could not afford friends, not yet, and probably not for a long, long time.

She became aware of the quickening steps and voices that were peculiar to the closing hours of any Friday. Even the whirr and slam of elevator doors seemed more distinct, heard now as not before, and in the air hung the feeling of everyone hurrying to leave.

There was nothing to hold her to her desk, but she sat on. The office was warm as her one-room, bathroom-down-the-hall apartment would not be, and she had nothing to hurry home to.

Stephanie set her lips in an uncompromising line. If beneath her veneer of cool sophistication there lay a mind at war with itself and a heart numbed by an almost fatal blow, it was none of the world's business. She had come to this city to forget the past — and she would.

A hollow quiet of emptiness settled

all about her. She could almost feel the building disgorging itself of human beings, and now she hurried too, getting into her coat without a glance at the mirror in the closetlike affair that was for her own private use.

Pocketbook under one arm, she pulled on her gloves, glanced about the office inspectively, and went down the wide hallway, glancing in at the open side door of Engineering. Everyone had gone. Then she was through the reception room and out the glass front door, its black lettering stating simply: Bayliss & MacArthur, Inc. Architects.

Emerging from the elevator into the lobby of the building, Stephanie paused to buy a magazine and permitted herself a brief moment of self-pity. It was raining outside, raining hard; street lights and headlights gave off a yellow glow in which rain danced with abandon.

The city had an air of celebration,

the work week ended, the passing faces eager. Stephanie felt out of things, as though life itself were passing her by. A great reluctance to leave the lobby to head for her cold, bare room descended upon her.

She made a mental survey of her financial condition. Payday was four days away; she had a little less than fifteen dollars to do her until then. To eat out would be an extravagance, but she could sleep late in the morning, get by with just one meal tomorrow. She certainly couldn't stand here in the lobby all night!

"Oh, well," she said, then hurried out into the rain as curious glances made her realize she had spoken aloud. Watch it, girl, she cautioned herself.

San Francisco is famous for its restaurants of every variety, and Stephanie thought of all the rich, gourmet food to be had as she turned in at a small café for a hamburger and coffee. She slid onto a stool at the counter and sat pulling off her gloves and enjoying the sudden heat after the cold rain.

She was just reaching for a menu when she heard her name spoken. She jerked around in surprise.

"Might as well join us, Mrs. Nelson," a heavy-set, handsome woman called out, and her companion, a sallow-faced blonde, smiled and nodded.

"Oh, hello . . . " Stephanie recognized them as fellow employees but could not think of their names. She had met most of the thirty-odd members of the company during her three-week stay. Now, with great reluctance, she joined the pair in the booth, murmuring, "I'm afraid I'm terrible about names."

"Carmen Foye, here," the stout woman said, "and this is Thelma McCullough. Your name is Stephanie, isn't it? We don't go in much for formality at B and M," she added with a smile.

Stephanie's smile felt stiff. Her eyes had swiftly taken in the thick steaks in front of them, and as a waitress approached she found she had not the nerve to order just a hamburger. "Medium rare," she told the waitress, hating herself for lack of courage.

"How do you like your job?" Thelma inquired.

"So far, I like it very much. Please, don't wait for me . . . " Stephanie gestured at their plates, whereupon they fell to with good appetite, looking pleased with her.

"You both work for Mr. Hubbard, don't you?" she asked, placing them now, and feeling resigned.

Nodding between bites, Carmen said proudly, "I've been with the company from the beginning, over six years now. Thelma, here, has been with us for over five years. What do you think of Liz Peterson?" she asked abruptly.

Stephanie frowned faintly. "She seems very pleasant. I haven't been with the company long enough to form definite opinions about anybody."

"I guess not." Carmen smiled. "It won't take you long to get acquainted."

"We were kind of surprised when they hired a young secretary," Thelma remarked. "Millicent Graves was sixty-five and retired. I guess we just got used to someone older."

Stephanie's food arrived, making it possible for her to avoid comment, but now Carmen was saying, "I understand you're a widow like me, Stephanie, and not a native."

Stephanie murmured a yes, hoping it would serve both questions, and she felt a tightening of nerves. The two opposite her were just friendly women with a natural curiosity about a newcomer, but she was not equipped yet to handle even idle questions.

"I do believe the rain has stopped," she remarked, for she faced the front. And she laughed thinly. "This is such a hilly city. I'm not yet used to the idea of it, but it is beautiful, I think." She knew she was talking merely to keep them from doing so, but she could almost see the questions they were waiting to ask. "Do you often

17

stay in town after work?" she asked as if she cared.

"We're going to a movie," Thelma said. "Want to come with us?"

"Thelma's fiancé is overseas," Carmen informed Stephanie, "so we kind of keep each other company, you know? It's a good picture."

"Thank you, but no, I'm expecting a call." She made a small business of inspecting her wrist watch. "Dear me, I should hurry."

Now on their dessert, the two women seemed to be sitting back and studying Stephanie at leisure. "Do you mind telling me who hired you, Stephanie?" Carmen asked.

"I beg your pardon? Oh. Why, Mr. Bayliss interviewed me," she said, wondering what difference it made and why the two were exchanging looks.

"Paul's a fine man," Carmen declared. "I've known him and Mac since the beginning. Knew Paul's wife, too. She died a couple of years ago, I guess you know."

"No, I didn't know. It's hardly something I would know, is it?"

"Surprised Liz didn't tell you, but, then, it's Mac she's after."

"Oh, Carmen, I don't think so," Thelma said, giving Stephanie a half-apologetic look.

"Well, Liz certainly wanted your job, Stephanie, you might as well know," Carmen said defensively.

Stephanie dabbed at her mouth with her napkin, gathered up her purse and gloves, and slid out of the booth. "Excuse me," she said. "I must hurry or I'll miss my call. Nice to have seen you."

They watched her as she paused to pay her check, then rush out of the café. "What do you think?" Thelma asked.

Carmen considered, shook her head, and passed a judgment that time would not alter. "Close-mouthed," she pronounced.

Heading homeward, Stephanie felt she had not handled herself very well.

It was too soon, she grieved. Her mind panicked under questioning. Not enough time had passed between her and the ordeal of the hearing. Give me time, she begged.

It hurt her inexplicably that Paul Bayliss was revealed as a widower. It explained his attitude, which was that they had both lost what was most precious to them.

And he's so wrong, Stephanie sighed. She had not loved Stan Nelson for a long time before he died. On the very night he died, she had told him she was through — and other things painful to recall.

Don't, she begged her mind. Don't think about it. It's over, done! You're free — free!

"Let me forget," she whispered. "Don't let the past touch me here . . . "

2

HER so-called apartment was merely one large room on the third floor of what had once been a mansion and was now chopped up into apartments. There was no elevator.

Oh Lord, Stephanie thought as she climbed the stairs. If this job just lasts, I'm going to find myself a decent place to live!

Letting herself into the dark room, she groped for the one lamp, because she could not bear the garish look the top light shed upon the place. She mused that she would have done better to have walked home and saved the fare *and* spared herself the encounter with Carmen and Thelma, for she had gotten soaked through just walking from the cable car to the house.

She began to regret the unfinished

meal she had left, not just the waste of money but because she was hungry and there was nothing to eat. A smallish alcove comprised the kitchen area and held a refrigerator and a two-burner hot plate, one burner of which was inoperative. The rest of the room held a bed, a lumpy armchair, two straight chairs, and a table. A tall lamp with a glass beaded lamp-shade stood by the armchair. The carpet was threadbare and long lost as to pattern.

Presently, wet clothes exchanged for pajamas, robe, and slippers, Stephanie pulled the armchair close to the heater and sat forward, both hands around the coffee mug for added warmth. And, slowly, a sense of rightness crept over her. Being alone seemed to be her natural state.

It was never that you preferred being alone, she thought idly; it was merely that you were used to it and did not mind it. For the briefest of times, just before and after her marriage to Stan, had she not felt alone, and that was now nearly five years ago.

But nothing could change the past; all one had was today and tomorrow and the hope of betterment. Certainly, her job with Bayliss & MacArthur seemed a good omen, for she had landed it within three weeks of arriving in the city and the job was far better than any she had held before.

It's just a matter of time, she reflected to comfort herself. Time heals every hurt or covers it over with layers of forgetfulness. Remember how you felt when you were taken from the home by the Smiths?

Stephanie did not remember her parents. She had, literally, been left on the doorstep of a fine children's home as an infant, a slip of paper pinned to her blanket with information: *Her name is Stephanie, eleven months old and sickly. Be good to her.*

At the home she was given the surname Smith, which was at least euphonious, and she had been well cared for. Leaving the home when

23

she was six had been traumatic. It had meant nothing to her that the strange man and woman made their choice by the coincidence of surnames. She was simply terrified.

Milford Smith was a quiet, ineffectual little man, who, long before Stephanie's arrival, had ceased to strive against his formidable big wife. He was kind at heart but as shy as the child herself, and over them both hovered the shadow of Luella Smith, devout churchwoman, stern moralist, rigid disciplinarian, who seemed quite devoid of those qualities that make women mothers.

It was then, Stephanie supposed, that she had learned the uselessness of crying. She was not abused physically; she was well fed and reasonably well clothed, but she was quite alone, a frightened child with no arms to hold her and comfort her.

Uncle Milford and Aunt Luella, as she was directed to address them, lived in a small town in upstate New York. Milford Smith managed a hardware store he dreamed of owning and never did; Luella Smith managed everything and everyone within hearing distance. And Stephanie moved like a wraith between them.

Uncle Milford tried to lessen her burdens, Stephanie remembered, for his wife was very strict with her and overworked her, but the bond of sympathy between them remained tacit.

Poor old Uncle Milford, Stephanie mused, and poor young me; neither of us with the guts to answer Aunt Luella back. But in the end, Uncle Milford had outwitted his wife by dying quietly and leaving her with a pile of debts of such magnitude her pride was broken. Within three months she had a stroke and died.

Stephanie by then had graduated from high school and was clerking in the hardware store and having wistful thoughts about college. She had been half planning to run away when Uncle Milford's treachery, as his wife called it, was exposed; she had stayed on out of a sense of duty to the little man who had shown her kindness and to help his big wife pay off his debts.

Aunt Luella's death freed Stephanie, for when the old house was sold all the debts were settled with a few hundred dollars left over. Stephanie took the money and left town, never to return.

She traded her dream of college for a decent business school in the big city, and completely alone, she discovered a strong determination to survive. She was eighteen, not unattractive, and intelligent. And not afraid of work.

Stephanie got up and refilled her coffee mug, a little smile tugging at her lips. If, except for Uncle Milford's shy little looks, she had known no love under his roof, she could look back now and realize that Aunt Luella's eternal vigilance lest 'that orphan girl' go astray had toughened something within her, something that had to do with self-reliance.

She had never made any real friends

during her twelve years with the Smiths. Aunt Luella had suspected every almost-friend until it was easier to forego the idea. But Stephanie had found favor with her teachers, and there had been some good times.

Stephanie Nelson looked back at Stephanie Smith and shook her head. There had never been any sense of family; she had always been 'that orphan girl.' She had never expected to be anything else.

And then, having completed business college and found a job as a typist in an advertising firm in Manhattan, she had met Stanley Nelson.

It was no wonder that, after years of emotional deprivation, she had fallen into his arms so easily. She had thought him the most wonderful person on earth, so handsome, so full of life and laughter *and* so in love with her! The miracle of it blinded her to everything else. She could not see the man for the stars in her eyes.

God, she thought, was I naïve! She

knew now what she had not known then — that he had married her because it was the only way he could have her, for too many years under Aunt Luella's stern guidance and church twice every Sunday had prevailed.

She had not wanted to elope, but she had not yet learned to express opinions with much force, and Stan had reminded her she had no family. There was nothing he did not know about her, so eager was she to communicate, leave nothing unsaid, unknown, between them.

Her lips twisted in self-derision as she remembered how little she had known about him. He had spoken of his parents and his sister, Maude, in glowing terms, but she had not met them. She remembered how nervous Stan had seemed on the way back from the weekend honeymoon and how she had misunderstood, reading it as excitement to be taking his bride home to his family.

She had not been nervous, she

reflected. She had blindly expected to be welcomed into the bosom of his family with open arms. It hadn't happened that way, but in the beginning she had blamed her own shyness.

Stan was the hub around which the lives of his parents and sister revolved. Maude, twelve years his senior and unmarried and unattractive, worshipped her little brother jealously; to his mother he was her baby boy who could do no wrong. To the elder Nelson, the son of his middle age was something of a miracle. If Mr. Nelson had never been overtly unkind to Stephanie, he had never approved of her.

Stan was a spoiled son and brother, good-natured, fun-loving, bad-tempered, sulky — all according to the atmospheric conditions around him. It made Stephanie careful in the first days. She did not complain of his family's dislike of her more than once, for it made him testy, and he blamed her that it was so.

All she had known about Stan when they married had seemed wonderful. He was a first-year law student with a job on the side, and she was thrilled to the marrow at the mere idea of being married to a professional man.

She kept her job, having by then graduated to the secretarial pool with a raise in pay, and she was determined to help Stan in every way possible and to make their small apartment an oasis in his busy life.

Great hopes were held for Stanley Nelson and great sacrifices made. Stephanie felt debased when she learned that his family financed his education and that the job he supposedly held was a myth. She fought disillusionment; she humored and cajoled Stan in emulation of his family for fear of losing him. She addressed envelopes by the thousand each evening to augment her own salary and keep Stan from mooching pocket money from his sister.

She fought a losing battle. By the time Stan flunked out of law school at the end of his second year, swearing her to secrecy where his family was concerned, she had lost all respect for him; but she hung on because failure in marriage loomed in her mind as a disgrace, a failure in herself.

I was a nag, Stephanie grimaced. Stan turned me into a nag. He was so absolutely irresponsible! I should have left him when he flunked out of law school. I'll never know why he did not leave me!

In a curious way, her husband's failures had spurred Stephanie's ambition for herself. In the four and a half years of her marriage, she polished her skills with something of the same determination with which Stan let his deteriorate.

She became assistant to the supervisor of the secretarial pool, making good money, but Stan's spendthrift ways tightened her purse strings and dedicated her to thrift. Stan jeered at her skinflint habits and was not above helping himself to money from her pocketbook.

He took jobs here and there, but they never lasted, and even when his family knew his law career was over, they blamed others, Stephanie in particular, for the failure.

Such a charming man, so popular with his peers, so sought after and admired, it had always amazed Stephanie. It had not amazed her that girls found him irresistible. She had herself, in the beginning. His physical appeal was great.

Her coffee now cold, Stephanie took the mug to the small sink and rinsed it, then just stood, letting the cold water run over her wrists. That one so gay and dedicated to fun should be dead seemed incongruous. Yet, she wondered, was it possible that Stan had had a secret contempt for life? He seemed in such a rush to get it over, never to stop to think, to look at himself.

But never, never, did I wish him dead, she thought painfully. I was wrong for him. He was wrong for

32

me. But he never really complained; he was incapable of quarreling. He'd just grin and grab up his hat and go off to join his friends.

He was a child. His family never let him grow up or wanted him to; that was all I did want. Stephanie turned off the water, dried her hands. Not his fault, her thoughts ran, and maybe not mine either. He couldn't help being what he was any more than I could help being what I was.

She turned off the gas heater and went to bed, wondering why she had let herself dwell upon the past tonight. It was dangerous; it could bring on the nightmare and the pounding of fists on her door.

Just a few nights before she had come screaming out of that nightmare, shaking and sweating and half blind with terror, and the tenants on the same floor had heard and come to investigate. She had done what was necessary for self-preservation: she had denied she had screamed, and shut the door on their staring faces.

I must move from here soon, she thought tiredly. If her job lasted, and it did seem as though it would, she'd find a nice apartment with a bathroom and a real kitchen, and she'd live nicely, quietly, and soon time would flow over the past and bury it.

Half asleep, she remembered what a co-worker back in the advertising firm had said of her a few short years ago: "She's a loner." And she had felt vaguely hurt, for although she was by nature retiring, she felt she was friendly.

But the supervisor of the secretarial pool had liked her. Liz Peterson of Engineering seemed to like her. It was nice to be liked.

Paul Bayliss liked her. But would he like her if he knew . . .

She shuddered her way into sleep.

3

PAUL BAYLISS' eyes softened on Stephanie's bent head as he dictated. He had liked her from the first moment she entered his office for the interview, and he was very pleased that she had proved so efficient.

Mac had demurred a bit when told the new secretary had no architectural experience, but even Mac now had to admit that Stephanie was fast becoming indispensable.

Such a sensible young woman, Paul reflected. Quiet, neat, and with just the right touch of aloofness. Quite pretty in the plain way he admired.

"That's all for now, I guess," he said presently. "No hurry on those letters, Stephanie. I know Mac's been keeping you hopping."

"I don't mind. I like being busy." Stephanie smiled at him warmly; he gave her a feeling of security. Getting to her feet, she was emboldened to add: "I can't tell you how much I appreciate your patience with me, Mr. Bayliss."

He dismissed this with a wave of his hand. "We appreciate your eagerness to learn," he said. "You've got everything running more smoothly around here than I can remember. Of course," he added quickly, "your predecessor was up in years and had slowed with time."

"Well, thank you," she said, smiling as she moved away. "I'm glad you're pleased." She was aware of his eyes following her. Her most pleasant moments were spent in his office.

As she was leaving, Liz Peterson was coming out of Engineering. "Oh, there you are," she said. "I was just wondering if you'd like to join me downstairs in the coffee shop."

Stephanie glanced at the wall clock. "Yes, I'd like that, Liz. Be with you in a minute." And she stepped back into Paul Bayliss' office to let him know she was leaving; MacArthur had not yet arrived.

"Another Monday, eh?" Liz grimaced as they caught an elevator, then she smiled and winked. She was quite tall, thin and graceful, and smartly dressed. Her features were irregular, but her smile was beautiful and her big blue-gray eyes expressive. Stephanie liked her chiefly because she had not shown the curiosity about her the others had.

"Well," Liz said, sitting at the counter, "you've been with us about a month now, Steph." She shortened the name with utter ease. "What's the verdict?"

Wincing inwardly at the word, Stephanie spoke rather hurriedly. "I like my job very much. So far, so good, I guess. Mr. Bayliss seems satisfied with my work. I don't know about Mr. MacArthur — "

"Mac thinks you're okay. He's a good guy, Steph. I *am* surprised you're still calling him mister, though."

"Actually, he sort of asked me not

to, but I can't get used to such, ah, familiarity."

"Maybe it's being from the East," Liz observed casually. "Out West we're more informal, I guess, and then, most of us have worked for B and M since its beginnings."

Stephanie's mind registered the fact that Liz knew she was from the East, but somehow it did not bother her. And she was distracted from mulling this, for Liz was saying, "Do you always wear your hair that way?"

She lifted a hand to her hair. Brown like her eyes, it was pulled straight back from a center part to a loose loop at the nape of her neck. "Yes," she said, "I have for years." She felt amused. "Why, Liz? Don't you like it?"

"It's okay, but I have an idea it makes you look older than you are." She shook back her own flaming tresses. "I have a terrific beautician if you ever want to do something about it."

"I might just take you up on that one of these days," Stephanie said, moved by Liz's frank kindness. "It's been less expensive to wear it this way, but I do get tired of it long."

"I spend half my salary keeping my mop this stunning red. Wait till you see Ginny this morning."

"I did see her."

"Wearing that turban?" Liz laughed. "The crazy kid gave herself a home permanent, and her hair, which is naturally curly, came out frizzed to a fare-thee-well."

"Oh, poor kid."

"Yeah." Liz narrowed her eyes slightly. "She thinks you're something else, Steph. Thinks you look mysterious." She dragged the word out and laughed. "The kid sees too many movies."

"She must," Stephanie murmured.

Liz frowned faintly. "You know, Steph, you're the first new employee we've had in a long time. Ginny's the newest and she's been here a year. We've got a pretty good bunch of gals, but someone new is bound to get talked over, you know? And bound to get an earful, too."

Stephanie felt Liz was trying to help, but she could think of nothing to say. Liz continued. "You've probably heard that I wanted your job, Steph, and it's true, but Mac talked me out of it. He convinced me I'm practically indispensable to Engineering, and I guess I would miss giving my boys a hard time." She laughed, showing an expanse of good teeth. "Every darned architect in there is married, though," she added. "Mac says it keeps me out of trouble."

Stephanie had noted the camaraderie that existed between Liz and Mac and tried not to remember Carmen Foye's comment. It was none of her business, she reflected. And she liked Liz Peterson.

As they returned to the office, Stephanie felt curiously accepted; Liz might possibly become a friend. Almost. It was too soon to do more than put one foot ahead of the other and try to be inconspicuous.

They met Mac on the elevator, and Stephanie thought he looked at her curiously; but he did no more than nod good morning, then devoted himself to banter with Liz.

"You know, honey," he said as they left the elevator, "the Queen Mother was asking about you the other evening. Long time no see. Why don't you give her a ring today? You know how she loves little tidbits of office gossip."

"Maybe I shall. How is she?"

"Fine. How about this evening, Liz? I can drop you off on my way home."

"Let me call her first." At Stephanie's desk, Liz gave him a head-shaking look. "I suppose you're too busy with the beautiful Tina to do more than drop me off?"

"None of your business. Just go see my esteemed mother and I'll buy you lunch tomorrow."

"Okay, will do."

"A deal, then. And get with that progress report, will you?"

"Slave driver. But for you, anything!"

41

Stephanie did not look at them. She had not opened her mouth and felt oddly embarrassed. When Mac followed Liz into Engineering, she sat frowning for a moment. She hoped what Carmen Foye had said about Liz was not true. She did not think Mr. MacArthur cared about anyone but himself.

Her frown would have deepened had she overheard the conversation taking place at Liz's desk. "Say, honey," Mac was saying, resting on the edge of her desk. "I just had a brain wave. Mother hasn't met Steph yet, so how about asking her to go along with you this evening?"

Liz shrugged. "I can ask her, Mac, but first I want to call your mother, see if she's free."

"She's free. I told her last night I'd ask you about this evening."

"Oh, you. I'll ask Steph," she repeated, "but I doubt if she'll accept."

"Why not?"

She frowned at the sharpness of his

tone. "Just because," she said patiently, "you can't expect her to understand this crazy company. You have to remember, she's new here, new to the city. And — and different."

He straightened. "Well, suit yourself, Liz," he said, moving away. "It was just a thought."

She regarded his departing wide shoulders with a half-quizzical look. She understood his brain wave, in part. His mother was a darling little woman who had suffered an accident the year before that had left her crippled. Before that, she had been a very active woman, and Liz knew how it hurt Mac and his sister, Beth, to see her confined to a wheelchair. Liz was a favorite of Mrs. MacArthur's.

But Steph? Liz frowned. Stephanie's predecessor had not been on familiar terms with Mac's mother, so why Stephanie? Oh, well, she thought, all I can do is ask, but I doubt if she will accept.

Later, Liz and Stephanie had lunch

together in the coffee shop, and once more one regarded the other with thoughtful eyes, then without preamble said, "Mac thinks his mother might enjoy meeting you, Steph. She's a nice old lady, crippled, in a wheelchair. Takes a lot of interest in the company. Are you busy this evening?"

Stephanie felt she was staring. "Why, I — " she began, frowned, and shook her head. Liz saw her bewilderment.

"It's okay," she said. "You don't have to go. I mean, it's not compulsory!"

Stephanie felt relief, yet somehow in the wrong, particularly when Liz dropped the subject. She could not tell about Liz's reaction; she worried about offending Mr. MacArthur, who didn't like her too well as it was.

"Liz," she said at last, "I was just surprised. I'll be glad to. I've never worked for a . . . a family business."

"It's hardly, that, Steph. Mac and Paul aren't related." Liz shrugged suddenly, understanding Stephanie's dilemma. "You'll like Mrs. MacArthur," she said consolingly, "and we won't stay long. Mac's a good son," she added rather defensively. "His father died a couple of years ago."

"I see. How do we get there?"

"Oh, Mac'll drop us off on his way home."

"He doesn't live with his mother?"

"No, he has his own apartment. His sister doesn't live far from his mother with her husband and kids, and Mrs. MacArthur has Greta." Liz grinned. "Greta is the housekeeper, and as Mac says, his mother's watchdog. You'll like seeing the house. It's old but beautiful, on Nob Hill."

When Stephanie returned to her desk she had a curious sensation, as though she were being drawn into a swiftly moving stream. She did not want to go with Liz after work. She did not want to meet a strange, high-born lady who lived on Nob Hill. She had heard of Nob Hill, or read of it. The whole idea frightened her.

In Paul Bayliss' office later, Stephanie

looked at him, measuring his regard for her. Because he had always been kind, she blurted, "Mr. Bayliss, may I ask you something?"

"Of course." Her troubled brown eyes touched him curiously. "Something wrong, Stephanie?"

"No — not really. Just something I don't understand."

He smiled. "If I can help," he said, "here I am." And she was able to ask his advice without too much faltering. "Well, now, Stephanie," he told her, "it's nothing to worry about. I understand your reticence, but you'll find Mrs. MacArthur a charming old lady. Actually," he added, "I've been neglecting her lately. If it would ease you, I'll give her a call and drive you out there after work."

Gratitude swelled within her, but she had to tell him: "Liz says Mr. MacArthur plans to drive us."

"Oh, that's all right. I'll speak to Mac." His nice gray eyes twinkled. "You do have a time using our first names, don't you?" he asked kindly.

"I'm afraid so."

"Well, don't worry about it. I'm afraid we are a bit lax about some things." He stood, regarded her warmly. "I suppose I should have asked you if you'd like me to drive you to Mrs. MacArthur's?"

"No, I appreciate it. And I do thank you . . . Paul."

"Well, fine." He looked extremely pleased. "I hope you'll feel free to bring any little problems to me, Stephanie. You are a . . . a very nice person."

Mac looked at her curiously as he passed her desk later to reach Liz. Paul had acted both embarrassed and a bit smug in revealing the new development. Not that Mac minded, but it rather worried him, for Paul's sake.

"Say, Liz," he said, reaching her, "a change in plans. Paul will drive you and Steph to my mother's place after work. Seems he was planning to go, anyway."

"Okay, did you tell Steph?"

"She knows," he said shortly and departed. Liz frowned. Just about the time she decided Mac really liked Stephanie, she had to change her mind. Paul certainly liked her, she thought with an odd sense of worry. Already in the company lounge there was talk about how much Paul seemed to like his secretary.

Liz's worry deepened on the way to the MacArthur house, for Paul was acting in a way that teased her mind. Was he really falling for Stephanie? And what about Stephanie? Actually, Liz mused, I don't know a darned thing about her!

Stephanie was struggling with butterflies in her stomach, but she was deeply grateful for Paul's presence and profoundly glad Mac would not be there. She hoped Mrs. MacArthur would not be intimidating in her aristocracy.

Althea MacArthur was a tiny woman with alert blue eyes in a still lovely face, and snow-white hair cut short in gentle waves. She sat very straight in her wheelchair and received her guests with warm pleasure, her eyes skimming Stephanie intently even before Paul introduced her.

"Yes, of course," she said, offering her hand. "Stephanie! What a lovely name! Hello, Liz, you wretch. Paul, it's been too long."

Stephanie relaxed slowly, for Liz did most of the talking, making the little woman laugh and the florid-faced housekeeper shake her head in a pleased way. From time to time, Stephanie felt the alert blue eyes upon her, but other than asking her how she liked her new position, Mrs. MacArthur did not press her.

The call was a short one, and presently Paul was driving again and saying, "I know where you live, Liz, but Stephanie will have to show me."

"Oh, you can drop me anywhere," Liz said, and something in her tone alerted Steph.

"I, too, Paul," she said quickly.

"Nonsense, I wouldn't think of it."

Stephanie did not want him to see where she lived, and she wished he would not keep glancing at her and smiling. What was he smiling about? And why was Liz suddenly so unsmiling and quiet?

Liz felt disgruntled. Paul bothered her, he was being so darned obvious, and Stephanie certainly didn't seem to mind. She was glad to leave the car first and she merely grunted in going.

Alone with Paul, Stephanie stiffened her lips, and when he reached her address she did not wait for him to alight and open the door for her, but hopped out and looked back at him nervously.

"Thank you — enjoyed — very nice of you," she gasped and hurried away.

Paul sat watching her hasty departure with an odd pang. Poor girl, he thought, she's embarrassed. It was not a very nice neighborhood. He did not like the idea of Stephanie living in it. She did not seem strong to him, and he felt a rush of protectiveness.

Poor girl, he repeated. So alone and unprotected, and brave in her grief. It did not seem right.

He did not realize that he was equating Stephanie with his dead wife, who had been a delicate, fragile creature, wholly dependent upon him.

He knew only that something about Stephanie Nelson moved him immeasurably, as no woman had since Elaine.

Was it possible that he could know such happiness again?

4

MAC contemplated the ceiling, drummed his fingers on the desk and whistled thinly. Then leaving Stephanie erect in her chair, he went over to inspect some drawings on the huge drafting table in front of the windows. Stephanie kept her eyes on her notebook.

Six weeks had passed and she felt secure in her job and flutteringly hopeful for herself. She got through lonely evenings because her days were busy, she and Liz were becoming good friends, and an apartment of her own was in the offing.

Mac came back, sat down and barked out dictation at high speed for two or three minutes, then fell silent, his eyes taking her in with faint mockery. He liked her no better than in the beginning, but he admitted some curiosity about her.

"Found an apartment yet?" he startled her by asking, for she had no idea he knew she was looking for one.

"Not yet, but I do have a lead."

"The one in the building where Liz lives?"

Her eyes demanded what business it was of his. She simply replied, "Yes."

"Liz is a good egg. Seems to think you're all right. Are you, Steph?"

She made a small shrugging movement, not answering and having no idea how her closed, quiet face irritated him. She simply had learned that to answer impossible questions was to encourage his talk. And his talk could tighten her nerves.

Mac finished dictating and waved her away, then sat scowling. He couldn't remember when any woman bothered him more. He hated her deadpan look, her damnable efficiency. If Paul were not so sold on her . . .

Alexander MacArthur swore under

his breath. Paul was ripe for remarriage, and in a subtle sort of way Stephanie resembled his dead wife. No, not really, he amended, except that Elaine Bayliss had had a sort of enigmatic quality about her until you got to know her, then pronounced her dull.

He did not think Stephanie was dull, just armored against attack. The thought surprised him, though not altogether, for his mother had evinced a sharp interest in Stephanie, declaring she just *knew* she had seen her somewhere before!

He had told his mother it was impossible, but he had not been able to forget her remark. Nor could he reconcile his mother's open liking for the girl with his own sense of distrust.

Liz Peterson's affection for Stephanie had deepened after a conversation they had had in the coffee shop. Liz worried that the talk about Stephanie and Paul might be true, and she did not like unnecessary worry.

"Say, Steph," she had remarked, "it's none of my business, so shut me up if you like, but I think you should know there's talk about you and Paul going around."

Stephanie had not been too surprised, but she had been wary of criticism. "I just hope such talk doesn't reach Paul's ears. He's been very kind to me, Liz, but that's all."

"Oh, I figured that," Liz said, relieved. "He is considered quite a catch," she added, "almost as much so as Mac."

Stephanie smiled. "I'm not interested, Liz. I like my life the way it is, or the way it will be when I find an apartment."

That was when Liz mentioned a possible vacancy in her building. She later reported to Mac that Stephanie was the least marriage-minded gal she knew, which had merely whetted his curiosity.

Leaving Mac's office and sensing his odd irritation, Stephanie felt slightly depressed. She did not know what he expected that she was not already producing. At times, his sleepy eyes seemed to hold an amused sort of liking for her, but usually they mocked her or were downright cold.

"What's the matter?" Liz asked, pausing in the doorway of Engineering. "Are they working you too hard?"

Stephanie managed a smile. "I'm just hungry," she said, "and not at all tempted by the sandwiches I brought with me."

"Didn't you get your check?"

"Oh, yes . . . "

"Well, let's splurge." Mac appeared in his doorway and Liz grinned at him. "How about it, Mac, you feel like taking two gorgeous gals to somewhere nice in Ghirardelli Square?"

"Not today, honey. Say, Steph, scrap that last letter, will you? I've decided to handle it in person. Have a good lunch, you two."

Liz grimaced, Stephanie felt relief. "Darn," Liz said. "I was hoping he'd take us to Chinatown. Well, let's go."

Stephanie shrugged, once again inwardly declaring the Liz-Mac relationship none of her business, but felt troubled by it nonetheless. Liz was outwardly so breezy and carefree, but no one knew better than Stephanie Nelson how a veneer could cover pain.

Ginny Goodwin looked up as Liz and Stephanie came through the reception room, her eyes admiring Stephanie, then rolling as Liz said: "Hi, kid. If Rock Hudson calls, tell him he's out of luck. I'm going steady with Mickey Rooney."

Laughter gushed from Stephanie, the sound surprising her with its rarity, and Liz looked pleased. Ginny continued to view Stephanie admiringly and inwardly planned to tell the "girls" that Stephanie was not snooty.

"I love your hair, Steph," she said.

"Oh, come on, Steph," Liz hooted. "The kid has no taste whatsoever."

Stephanie laughed again, this time experimentally. When they had first met, Stan had said he liked her laugh. At just what point had she forgotten how — until now?

At lunch, Liz regarded her companion with an edge of impatience. Not only did she deplore her hairdo, but Stephanie was procrastinating about the apartment.

"Better make up your mind soon," she said in regard to the latter. "I have an *in* with the landlord, but he won't hold it for long. If you don't want it, I know someone who does . . . "

"I want it," Stephanie said quickly, even as her mind argued against an apartment just doors from Liz. She had been putting off a decision for this reason.

"Good," said Liz. "Why don't you come home with me after work and cinch the deal?"

"All right. Thanks, Liz — "

"I wish I could get Sybil Knox to take that apartment, so you could move in with me. Not that I have anything against Syb, but we haven't much in common. She wouldn't do it, though, because she likes us sharing a front apartment."

Stephanie let her breath out slowly in gratitude to the young woman who shared Liz's apartment. She liked Liz better than anyone she had ever met, but she could never live with her — or anyone.

"Once you get moved in," Liz was saying, "*and* if you really want to scotch the talk about you and Paul, you should let me fix you up with a date."

"Oh, I don't think — "

"Why not? I know a fellow who'd be nuts about you. He's too short for me, but an all-right guy, Steph. I wouldn't steer you wrong. He's kind of a swinger, got lots of money, and not about to get serious, you know?"

"Well, I'll see."

"I'll give Jack a call, see what he's doing these days. And, if you don't like him I'll have Gary scare up some dates."

Stephanie laughed for the third time,

but now with an edge of nervousness. Once again, she felt as though she were being swept into a fast stream. "You've mentioned Gary before," she said quickly. "Is he your . . . ?"

"Nope," said Liz with a grin. "I've known him for years, knew his wife, and lent him my shoulder to cry on when the ingrate walked out on him. You'll like him, Steph, but Jack Ripley is a real fun date."

Fun. The word slid over her tongue with alien taste. Stan must have been a fun date to his girlfriends. Stephanie's chin came up. Why not? she thought. I'd like to know what it is to have fun, real fun. And I do feel bad about the talk linking me with Paul.

Within a week, she had left her dingy room behind and with it some of her fears. A place of her own absorbed her, and just as she had once made an attractive home for Stan out of a small apartment, now she threw herself into a redecorating project that had Liz amazed.

"You should have been an interior decorator, Steph," she said. "Wow! The colors slay me. I can hardly recognize the place already."

"Oh, but I have so much more to do. The landlord has given me permission to paint, do anything I want." She laughed. "So long as I pay for it, of course!"

Liz reported this new development to Mac. "Lord, I never saw anyone so excited about fixing up a one-bedroom apartment in my life. You know, Mac, it gave me a queer feeling. She has a real flair for color and isn't afraid to use it."

"Why a queer feeling, Liz?"

"I don't know." She had delivered a set of blueprints to him and was lingering, elbows propped on his drafting table. "She's just so excited!"

Mac tried to imagine an excited Stephanie and failed. "Well, it's nice she's satisfied. Move, will you?"

Liz moved a foot, frowned in an absorbed way. "It's like seeing a different side of her," she went on. "I keep feeling she's had bad breaks. I identify with her, Mac."

"Seems to me you're a bit obsessed," Mac said, trying to concentrate on his work. "I thought you preferred the company of men to women."

"I do, ordinarily." Liz laughed shortly. "Not that I'm in Steph's company much. She really is a loner — and lonely, Mac. Do you know? There isn't a single photograph, not even a photo album, in that whole apartment. And she never gets any mail."

"Liz, why don't you get back to work?"

"Why don't you like her?"

"I like her, I like her."

"You don't know her," Liz said stubbornly. "And I don't understand you, Mac. When I remember how good you were to me, practically saved my life . . . "

"Oh, come off it!"

"Well, you did. I was starving, literally starving, and when I passed out on the steps of the old building, you picked me up and — "

"Liz, for God's sake!"

"Well, you did. You got a doctor, you fed me, you gave me a job — "

"You were just a kid, Liz. Not quite eighteen. Steph's no kid."

"But she is alone and she hasn't any friends. Just me. I'm her only friend and I just know she's lonely. Every now and then when she laughs — "

"She can *laugh*?"

She elbowed him. "Don't be like that. Just because she's all business here doesn't mean she's really that way."

"Okay, Liz, have it your way, but get out of here, will you? I'm busy!"

She moved away, paused, then turned and touched his arm. "Mac, just one thing?"

"Just one thing, then out!"

"You remember the day Paul took Steph and me to the Queen Mother? Well, don't hit me, but I got the darndest feeling about Paul. I couldn't figure out what it was until later. Remember how sort of protective and fussy he was with his wife? Well, that's how he was with Steph."

Mac bent his head over his work. "So?"

Liz grinned. "I've had a sneaking suspicion that you've been sort of worried about it. Paul is such an open book. But you don't have to worry. Steph isn't interested!"

Mac slid his eyes around at her, denying an inner sense of relief. He knew her history, this big-hearted girl, and her vulnerability, her trusting nature.

"Liz, honey," he said, "what you need is a husband and some kids to mother. I have an idea you have a blind spot about Steph. Now, I like her. I've nothing against her. She may be all you say, but she isn't like you, honey, so don't attribute your own good heart to her."

"I wish you liked her more."

He chucked her under the chin.

"I'm nuts about her. Now, will you scram?"

She pushed his hand aside. "Just maybe," she declared, "you like her more than you know!" And she stormed out, for once out of patience with him. Mac shook his head after her. She was as bad as his mother when she got an idea in her head, and he was getting pretty sick of hearing about Mrs. Stephanie Nelson.

Stephanie Nelson herself was quite unaware of the interest in her. She went about with a preoccupied air, wondering if she could afford new draperies *and* a blender out of her next pay check. She really had to be thinking about a spring wardrobe.

The spring wardrobe was a must, particularly since she had committed herself to a blind date with that swinger, Jack Ripley. The thought of it was an annoyance. Her job and her apartment were enough for the moment.

But she had promised Liz, and whenever she thought of Liz her heart swelled in gratitude, not only for having gotten her the apartment, but because Liz did not make it a habit to run in and out without invitation. She was a wonderful friend.

Things were changing. Stephanie felt it in her bones. Not once had the nightmare troubled her here. And it was so exciting to work at making her apartment beautiful. Her very soul hungered for beauty. She could postpone fun very easily, she thought. After that dingy room, her apartment was heaven!

Liz had rather hoped for the usual running back and forth that existed when friends lived close by, but some inner wisdom cautioned her where Steph was concerned, so she was careful not to intrude. She had, however, a project that involved Steph . . .

She revealed it one evening when Stephanie invited her to dinner. A month had passed and the apartment was ready for a real showing. Stephanie was surprised by her eagerness to have it viewed and Liz was an enthusiastic audience.

"Not only should you have been an interior decorator, Steph, but you could have become that oddity — a lady chef. This meal is out of this world!"

"Liz, you're too generous." They were having coffee in the living room and her eyes moved about critically. "That chair," she grieved, "is impossible. I got a book out of the library about needlepoint and I'm determined to learn. I know just how I'd like to cover that chair . . . "

"You ought to go see Greta Hansen. Both she and Mac's mother are big on needlepoint."

"Oh, I couldn't do that."

"Why not? Steph, you don't understand about Mac's mother. She's crazy about young people and there's no one nicer."

"You've known her a long time, haven't you?"

"I lived at her house for a month once."

"You what?"

"It's true. I had my eighteenth birthday there. Seems a long time ago." Liz let her eyes consider Steph for a moment. "I left home when I was just seventeen, home in dear old Kansas on a dirt farm. My mother died and my stepfather remarried within the space of one month, so I took off. Bummed my way West . . . "

Stephanie listened with eyes averted as Liz told of dangers and escapades before she reached San Francisco with less than a dollar in her pocket.

"I saw an ad in the paper for a file clerk," Liz said, shaking her head. "I'd always dreamed of working in an office. I walked and I walked — you do know that B and M have just been in our present building for the last two years? Well, it's so. The old building was practically in the suburbs. I got there, and dumb me, I fainted on the steps as I was going in. Mac picked me up, called a doctor who pronounced me a starvation case, and next thing I knew the Queen Mother was hovering over me."

Stephanie was quiet, afraid the confidence was a prelude to reciprocity, and when Liz was silent, she did not know what to say.

"Mac gave me the job," Liz said, "and has big-brothered me ever since."

Stephanie came out of herself, distracted by a feeling of relief she did not stop to pinpoint. "I've noticed you and Mac seem good friends," she said.

"Oh, sure."

"More coffee?" She got up hurriedly and refilled their cups, her mind seeking a change of subject. "Liz," she said when she had reseated herself, "I've been wondering about what to wear on my blind date."

"It took you long enough to accept it. Well, let's see. He'll probably take you somewhere ritzy and your new things are pretty much officey. Why not splurge and buy something super?" Liz was beginning to grin. "And while

69

you're at it, how about doing something about your hair?"

Stephanie laughed. "I was wondering when you'd get around to that."

"I've been working on it subtle-like. Well, what about it?"

Stephanie looked around her living room and sighed. "Maybe I should do something about myself to match this room," she conceded.

"Hurrah for our side!" crowed Liz. "I'll call my hairdresser in the morning!"

Stephanie shook her head, bemused. "You know, Liz, you're quite a wonderful person."

"Yes, I am, aren't I?" Liz felt ridiculously vindicated and elated at the success of her project. "Listen," she said, earnestly then, "if you don't like Jack Ripley, Steph, don't worry. Gary has a friend — "

"Oh, Liz."

"And Gary has a cousin who's coming out here on a visit. We can double-date. Let's go shopping tomorrow after you have your hair done. I can't wait to see how you'll look!"

Stephanie was laughing. It was easier than crying, which was what she felt like doing. Oh, Liz, Liz, she thought, if I could tell anyone, it would be you, but I can't, I can't risk losing your friendship.

5

MAC did an exaggerated double take when he arrived at the office two mornings later.

"I say, Miss, you're new, aren't you?" he inquired with mock seriousness. "Whatever happened to the widow woman we used to have?"

Stephanie laughed. She had been basking in compliments from all sides and somehow Mac's approval seemed important.

"I think," she said brightly, "the woman you refer to was last seen entering a beauty salon on Market Street."

Mac's mind recorded the laugh. "Let's hope," he said lightly, eyes narrow, "she never shows her face around here again."

Stephanie looked away, suddenly self-conscious. "A Mr. Rutledge of

Apex Construction called," she said, swiftly the secretary. "Shall I get him back for you?"

"Sure, go ahead." Mac moved on to his office, feeling disappointed. Just for a minute there, she had seemed almost human!

Paul Bayliss had complimented Stephanie on her new coiffure, but inwardly had felt a pang of loss. Stephanie looked far too young to him now; he had thought of her as a woman, and this morning she wore the face of a girl.

Liz, of course, went about looking as if she had invented Stephanie and was about to take out the patent. And she did not forget to hint in the lounge that Stephanie was dating a very special man, an exaggeration, since her blind date was not until that night.

It was a heady experience for Stephanie. She had told Liz she didn't care how her hair looked, it *felt* so wonderful, but she was not immune to flattery and she felt the cutting off of her long hair was a step in the right direction.

The day became eventful. Mac went off to the construction site of a new project and wasted so much time teasing Steph beforehand, he forgot an important set of specifications.

Stephanie answered the phone. "Of course, Mac, I know where they are. You want them sent out to you?"

"You bring them out, Steph," he told her. "About time you saw what it's all about."

She was, by now, knowledgeable about projects planned, underway, and near completion, and she often pored over sketches and drawings, but she had never seen an actual construction. She felt her heart leap with eagerness, but all she said was, "Very well, Mac," and hung up.

She went in to tell Paul where she was going and although she spoke crisply, her brown eyes belied her tone. Paul looked at her thoughtfully.

"I suppose Mac is right," he said.

"I'm sorry I didn't think of it myself, Stephanie. Seeing our work made a reality can be very exciting."

For a moment, she was sorry it was not he who had arranged the brief trip. "You're sure my going won't inconvenience you?" she asked anxiously.

"No, you run along. You have the address?"

"Oh, yes, Mac gave it to me."

"Well, call a cab. Have Ginny give you some money out of petty cash."

"Oh, I don't mind — "

"Now, Stephanie, this is business."

"All right." She gave him the warmth of her smile. "Mac didn't say how long I'd be, Paul."

"No matter. I have an appointment with the law firm that will keep me out till mid-afternoon. Enjoy yourself, Stephanie. I just wish I were the one who . . . "

She hurried away, excitement dashed by his remark. Perhaps it was just as well it was Mac she was to meet. At least no one would talk about her where he was concerned!

It was a lovely day, the city freshly washed with springtime sunshine. She was glad she had worn one of her new spring outfits. She felt young and a little silly, and as the taxi bore her toward her destination, she put the thought of Paul Bayliss aside and let excitement have its way.

Mac's eyes took her in narrowly as he paid the driver. Hey, his mind recorded, she's darned near beautiful today!

"I had money to pay him," she was saying and laughing a little, then, "Oh, Mac, it's going to be beautiful!"

He took the specifications from her, saying, "Go ahead, look around, Steph. I won't be long."

She nodded, eyes everywhere. The construction underway would emerge as a library, much needed in this outlying district, and already it was taking form. She felt a thrill to know it a Bayliss & MacArthur creation.

Her questions were intelligent, Mac thought when he returned to her. He was amused and rather touched by the proud eagerness she showed, and he laughed at her openly expressed envy of his talents and that of the other architects.

"It's absolutely fascinating," she said, quite without self-consciousness in her delight. "It must make you feel like a sort of god to see the creation of your mind emerging as a reality."

"If you only knew the dreams I used to have of creating cathedrals," he laughed.

"Did you always want to be an architect?"

"Always. Ask my mother."

Stephanie's attractive laugh rang out, but at the mention of his mother, her eyes looked away from him, and she was pleased to leave the site, getting into his car when he so bade her.

"My," she said, looking at her wrist watch, "I didn't realize the time."

"Time to put on the feed bag," he

said, driving away. "I have one stop to make, Steph, then I'll buy you a sandwich."

Well, she thought, he was the boss and it was a lovely day. "Whatever you say," she said, and added, with boldness for her: "You're the boss."

He grinned. "And don't you forget it." And when she laughed, he added, "You know, Steph, you ought to laugh more often. Anybody ever tell you what a pretty laugh you have?"

She did not know what to say, and Mac cast her an amused look. He wondered what Paul thought of her new image.

"How long have you been with us now, Steph?"

"Just over two months. Somehow," she said idly, "it seems longer. Because of Liz, I think."

"Oh? How so?"

"Hard to say. She's quite a wonderful person."

"Yes, she is. I think the world of Liz."

She felt an odd little pang and wondered at it. Her nature was not jealous, so it could not be that. Then Mac was saying, "Paul thinks you're pretty wonderful yourself, Steph."

Again, she did not know what to say, for there was a slight edge to his tone, but she was distracted, for she realized they were approaching his mother's house.

She slid down deeper in the seat, glancing at him questioningly, but he seemed unaware of her. Stopping the car in the driveway, he reached across her and took a flattish package from the glove compartment. Then he got out of the car and walked around and opened her door.

"Oh," she gasped, "that's all right. I'll just wait here."

He seemed to hesitate for a second, then turned brusque. "Don't be silly!"

"But I don't mind waiting."

"My mother would mind. Come along, girl. If we're lucky, Greta may feed us."

She moved stiffly by his side, then stood back when he pushed the front door open and shouted, "Mother? Greta?" He shrugged. "They must be in the kitchen. Come on, Steph."

His shouts brought the housekeeper to the kitchen door, saying over her shoulder, "It's Alex, of course, Thea, who else is ever so noisy — " She gave Steph a half-startled look. "It's Alex with Mrs. Nelson," she added.

Althea MacArthur, too, seemed briefly startled, but greeted Stephanie warmly. "How nice! You won't mind taking potluck with us, will you? Greta, dear, set plates for them. Alex, please, don't shout!"

Mac made a big thing of explaining how Stephanie happened to be with him as he gave his mother the package. "She's a nut on mysteries," he added to Stephanie. "Keeps me broke finding her new ones."

Stephanie did not mind his noise. The more he talked the less she needed to, and she had lost her nervousness, for the two women accepted her presence without fuss, his mother quickly finding a subject to ease her.

"I hear you've moved into an apartment near Liz," she said. "She came by last Sunday and did a lot of raving about your homemaking talents, Stephanie. She said something about you wanting to learn needlepoint."

"Yes, I'm making a stab at it. You see, I have this horrible chair . . . "

Mac listened as the three women waxed enthusiastic about needlepoint and quite ignored him. Briefly, he regretted bringing Stephanie here, then consoled himself with the thought that his mother loved young visitors.

They left him to his own devices after lunch while they went off to inspect chairs that were done some years before, and when he finally announced it was time to leave there was a general show of reluctance.

Stephanie looked at him as though she wondered what he was doing there, then was quickly embarrassed, a faint

81

tinge of coral brushing her cheekbones. Mac stared, thinking her lovely.

"Now, dear, you must come back soon. And bring your needlepoint," his mother was saying.

"It's not hard to learn," Greta added, "and it's wonderful that you can plan your own design."

"Thank you, thank you," Steph was saying a little breathlessly, and she did not look at Mac as he hurried her away.

"I can't get over it," Althea MacArthur said when the young ones were gone. "Greta, where have we seen that girl before?"

"I haven't," Greta said, and frowned. "I did rather think the first time we saw her that she was much like Elaine Bayliss was at that age, but I couldn't see any resemblance today."

"I wish I could think," the other complained. "I must be getting old, for I *know* I've seen that face."

Greta shook her head. "Well, you'll worry it until you do remember, Thea,"

82

she said, then laughed softly. "Alex was embarrassed," she added.

Althea, too, laughed. "Yes, he always gets so noisy when he's embarrassed, but it doesn't have to mean anything."

"No, no, of course not, but . . . "

They were very old friends and both now widows. Greta Hansen had been the MacArthur housekeeper so long she was a member of the family; childless, she had mothered the MacArthur children and now did the same for the MacArthur grandchildren. No line defined mistress and housekeeper.

"But what, Greta?" Althea asked now.

"I was just thinking about Paul, and how we thought he was attracted to Stephanie. And, now, today, Alex bringing her here . . . "

"Oh, dear, that would be dreadful."

"Yes, let's not even consider it. Stephanie was with Alex by sheer coincidence, and he did promise you that book he brought."

"Yes, yes, and, besides, Greta, Alex

and Paul have never been attracted to the same type of girl."

"What's this?" Coming in the back way, Mac's sister eyed the two women with quick suspicion.

"Oh, Beth! Nothing, dear. Did you find the cheese Greta wanted?"

Beth set a carton of groceries on the kitchen table where the two were sitting. "Everything on your list is there, Greta," she said, and sat. She was a strikingly beautiful young woman, who did not look four years older than thirty-one-year-old Mac *or* the mother of two teenagers. "All right, you two," she demanded, "just what is this about Alex and Paul being attracted to the same girl?"

"Beth, we said nothing of the sort," her mother scolded.

"No? Who was the girl I saw with Mac just now?"

"You saw them?"

"Just a glimpse as he drove away, but enough to know it *was* a girl."

"It was his secretary. They were out

84

at some construction site on business, and Alex just came by to bring me a new book."

Beth's brown eyes sparked. "Aha, the new secretary! And a young one, at that! *And* my little brother bringing her here!"

"Now, Beth, don't you tease Alex about it." Beth and Alex loved each other, she was sure, but they had never been close. And Beth was such a tease! Althea looked to Greta, who was putting the groceries away, for help.

"It was nothing, Beth," Greta said. "Alex could hardly have left Mrs. Nelson sitting in the car. And she seems a very nice young woman."

"*Mrs.* Nelson?"

"She's a widow, dear," Althea said, and she knew her daughter too well to hope to distract her now. "Actually, Beth, Greta thought Stephanie rather resembled Elaine Bayliss when we first met her, but not today."

Beth looked happy. "I see," she said. "So that's why you were mentioning

85

Paul. It's about time he married again. I always liked Elaine and if this secretary is anything like — "

"We didn't say she is. She's not anything like Elaine was. I always thought Elaine rather dull."

"I know, Mother. You and Alex, both. But, tell me more about this Mrs. Nelson."

"There's nothing to tell. Paul brought her to see me sometime ago — "

"Aha!"

"Oh, Beth, stop that aha-ing," her mother said crossly. "Isn't it about time you were picking your children up at school?"

"No, it isn't, Mother mine," Beth laughed, but she got to her feet. "All right," she said, "but you've whetted my curiosity. I'm going to have to take a look at this new secretary. Is she pretty? She'd have to go a long way to outshine Tina Marshall."

Her mother sighed. "Beth, you are a tease," she said. "You and Bob, I remember, teased Alex unmercifully."

Beth's face sobered. "I still miss him, Mama," she said.

"Yes, I know, dear," her mother said, sorry to have cast this shadow over her daughter. Beth's twin brother had died years before.

Greta sought to lighten the mood. "My, Beth, you and Bob were a pair, all right. Never in my life did I ever see such beautiful twins — and so inseparable. People used to stare."

"They did, didn't they? I often think that, if Bob had lived, I should never have married."

"You had not met Thorn then, dear," her mother said, vaguely troubled. "Thorn is a fine man."

"I know that. I love him. But I still miss Bob . . . "

After Beth left the two women sat in silence for some time, and then Althea sighed aloud. "She's never been the same since Bobby died," she said, "I thank God for Thorn. Beth and Bobby were almost too close."

"She's a good girl, Thea. She doesn't

mean half she says."

"You're right, of course. I just hope she forgets about Stephanie Nelson." Althea stared at her hands. "Greta," she added, "you don't really think it was significant, do you?"

"Alex has never brought any other girl, except Liz, to this house, but no, I don't think it was significant."

"But he was embarrassed."

They sat on in silence.

6

STEPHANIE found Jack Ripley the most amusing of companions and was vastly relieved, for she had had her doubts about a blind date. If there was something superficial about him, it pleased her; she wanted no serious note to enter into the night.

He took her to dinner at Ernie's, a fine restaurant that specialized in Continental cuisine, and then to the theater, and when he left her at her apartment door, he made a date for two nights hence. Then he kissed her on the nose.

Alone, Stephanie laughed to herself and her sense that things were changing deepened. Jack, she mused, was just what the doctor ordered. In his thirties, he had been married a couple of times and was now sworn off, which suited her fine. And while he had a job of sorts, he appeared to be independently well-off.

He was *fun*. And so she told Liz, who made a point of discussing the date in the lounge.

Carmen Foye, not liking ever to be wrong, said to Thelma, "I still say Steph has her eye on Paul. That's nothing but a cover-up."

Paul Bayliss had not yet analyzed his feeling for Stephanie. He was a little put off at the idea of Stephanie living so close to Liz, whom he considered likeable enough but a bit common. Still, he felt that Stephanie turned to him when any problem troubled her.

He had reassured her over her visit to Mrs. MacArthur with Mac, saying, "I felt that Mrs. MacArthur liked you the day I took you there, and I'm very glad you saw her again. Anytime you'd like to go back, just let me know, Stephanie. I'll be happy to escort you."

Stephanie was much at ease with him, and she knew no way to visit

Mrs. MacArthur alone freely. She very much wanted Greta's help with the needlepoint; however, the idea of going anywhere with Paul was a worry. She felt he was too high-minded to realize that talk could ensue.

Mac watched Stephanie with growing approval and felt easier about Paul. Liz did not fail to report her friend's social activities to Mac, having taken a proprietary interest in her progress.

"I figure she's over her husband's death now," she told Mac. "And she's having a ball. She could date every night in the week if she wanted to."

"Good for her."

"You do like her, don't you?"

He rolled his eyes. "I'm madly in love with her."

Liz sighed. "Well, your mother is crazy about her, Mac. We were out there the other evening, did you know?"

"No." Mac frowned, face averted. "But you'll always be Mother's favorite, honey."

"I know that. Well, be seein' you."

It was well into April now and Mac felt restless. Tina was giving him a bad time, accusing him of losing interest, and he did not want it to be so.

He looked at Stephanie obliquely one afternoon as she sat waiting for him to dictate. She had changed a lot, he reflected. She must be spending as much as Liz on clothes and trappings of beauty. He applauded the idea, but she still bothered him. Even Liz did not seem to know much about her past.

At that moment Stephanie was remembering how Mac had likened January to springtime on his birthday. She now appreciated him for his near-genius talent and she felt that he no longer disliked her. She tried very hard to be liked, laughing at his jokes and even attempting small jokes herself.

Unexpectedly, she yawned, and Mac's eyes swung to her, his grin much in evidence. "Son-of-a-gun, Steph, I swear you get more human every day."

She laughed. "Because I yawned?

It's too warm in here and you have a penchant for long silences that are a bit soporific."

"Pretty words."

Her brown eyes inspected him. "When I first came to work here I thought you were the laziest man in my experience."

"And I thought you were a pain in the neck."

"I know," she said, and for a moment, eyes meeting, they were both laughing, then almost at once, were unaccountably embarrassed. Mac began to dictate very fast and Stephanie sat erect, her head bowed over her notebook. Afterward, separately, they both puzzled over the incident and wondered about it. And forgot it.

Liz accosted Stephanie as she was leaving Mac's office. "You remember me mentioning a cousin of Gary's coming here for a visit?"

"Faintly."

"Well, he was delayed, went to Los Angeles first, but he's here now. Or is arriving this evening. Gary and I are meeting him at the airport. Gary thought maybe the four of us could get together later. I hope you're free."

Through the doorway Mac listened with interest, hoping Steph would not close the door.

"Gosh, Liz, I'm sorry," she was saying, "but Jack has tickets for that new show and I just couldn't break our date. Why can't we get together tomorrow night?"

"Well, if you can't make it tonight . . . "

"Gary will probably want to visit with his cousin, anyway, don't you think? What's the cousin's name again?"

"Glen. Glen Hollander. I hope you like him."

"And if I don't?"

"Then I'll take him and you can have Gary."

Mac listened to Stephanie's burst of laughter. The merry widow, he thought, is waxing merry, all right. He felt disgruntled and got up and shut the door with a disapproving bang.

Liz and Stephanie glanced at the door, and Stephanie frowned. "I guess we were disturbing him," she said.

"Too bad about him. Well then, it's all set. I'll tell Gary's cousin he has a blind date tomorrow night."

"Okay, but I doubt if it will be very successful, Liz. Jack is the only blind date you've talked me into that I really enjoy."

"Oh well, if you don't like Glen, we'll all be together, so we can still have fun."

The following morning, Saturday, Liz knocked at Stephanie's door looking less than her cheerful self.

"Hi," she said. "We're out of coffee, Stephanie. Can you lend us enough for breakfast?"

"Sure. Sit down, Liz. Have a cup."

"Gladly. Sybil makes lousy coffee and I can't make it at all."

Steph regarded her with amusement. "What's the matter, Liz? Too much night life?"

"Not so you'd notice."

"Oh say, I forgot. Gary's cousin. Did he get here?"

"Oh, sure."

"Well? What's he like?"

"He doesn't look anything like Gary. Must be six foot three, at least. You know, tall, dark, and handsome."

"He sounds all right. Kind of tall for me." Steph laughed briefly. "What is it, Liz? You seem bothered about something."

"No, nothing." Liz helped herself to more coffee, eyes averted, and Steph frowned.

"All right, Liz, what is it? Come clean," she said, affecting humor. "Just what did happen last night?"

"Not a thing, honest. Gary and Glen talked a blue streak about the old days. They hadn't seen each other for years."

"Is Glen older or younger?"

"Younger."

"What does he do? He's from Los Angeles, right?"

"No, he just came here from Los

96

Angeles, but he's a New Yorker. He was with some law firm back there, but his mother died and he decided to move out West. I guess he's been looking different places with an idea of opening his own office."

Stephanie's mind had stopped on the words '*New Yorker*' and '*law firm*'. Liz was continuing, "He really appreciates us getting him a date right off."

"What did you tell him about me?"

"Just that you're gorgeous and he's sure to fall in love with you."

"Oh, Liz."

"Could happen," Liz said with a trace of wistfulness. "Anyway, he is real interested. There must be something about widows that men find irresistible."

Stephanie was already regretting the blind date. It was hardly conceivable that out of the millions of New Yorkers this man could be anyone who had known about the case. It had been over so fast.

"By the way, Liz," she said. "Don't

count on me for the whole weekend. Jack has something up his sleeve for tomorrow."

For a moment, Liz seemed to brighten. "That's okay. You really like Jack, don't you?"

"He's fun."

"This Glen seems sort of serious."

"Well, I told you blind dates are risky, but don't worry about me, Liz. I'll enjoy myself. Where are we going?"

"Somewhere nice, I'm sure. Glen will want to impress you."

Stephanie laughed, while measuring coffee from a cannister. "Here, friend," she said, and Liz stood up with a grimace.

"Forgot about old Sybil, and she's mad because it was my turn to shop. Thanks, Steph. See you later."

Stephanie saw her out, wondering about her unusual mood. Liz was always so bright-eyed and bushy-tailed in the morning. Maybe she didn't like this cousin of Gary Hollander's and was worrying about tonight.

Liz carried the coffee to her apartment and delivered it to the waiting Sybil, troubled because she hadn't been able to tell Stephanie what had happened. Not that anything *had* happened, except inside her, which was why it was hard to tell.

She did not understand it. When Glen Hollander had looked down at her from his formidable height and said, "Now I know I'm going to like San Francisco," something had turned over inside of her.

Once, when she was twenty, a man had swept her off her feet. After what she took to be a whirlwind courtship, he had catapulted her into a small private hell by revealing himself a married man.

Mac had helped Liz put the pieces back together, and for the almost four years since, she had shied away from emotional involvement. She was looking for love, but not impatiently. Once burnt, twice shy, was her credo.

And this morning she longed for Mac

to explain this feeling of derailment. It was pretty ridiculous. Just because a man was more than tall enough and had looked at her with fine dark eyes and held her hand in meeting a shade too long.

Glen Hollander. Liz swore softly. She hadn't been able to think of anything else since his first touch, and it made her feel crazy, and afraid. She wished she had told Stephanie, since she knew she wasn't interested in meeting Glen, or any man, but just the same, it gave her a queer feeling just thinking about Glen and Stephanie together. Stephanie was so pretty, so aloof, and so charming when she laughed, Glen would be sure to fall for her.

She had been so quiet the night before, Gary had asked her what was wrong, but she had said nothing, though she felt like crying like a baby. She had too much pride to tell Gary, and she had not been able to tell

Stephanie. Hey, Mac, she addressed his image, I may be heading for another downfall!

Gary Hollander was, at the moment, looking at his cousin with a blend of amusement and curiosity as they idled over breakfast. "Why all the interest in Liz, Glen? Stephanie Nelson is your date for tonight."

"I like Liz," Glen said. "And you went out of your way to say there's nothing serious between you."

"I think the world of Liz. She's no ordinary girl, so don't get any ideas."

"Are you telling me hands off?"

"I'm just saying she's something special and not so cocksure as she looks." Gary had sensed his cousin's reaction to Liz the night before and was wary of it. He felt that Glen was just a mite too handsome and probably used to women falling all over him.

Glen got up and walked about. "I just said I liked her, Gary. Not often I meet a girl tall enough. I'm not about to try to steal her from you."

"You'll like Steph." Gary did not know why he felt so wary. Something subtle, tacit, had happened between Liz and Glen last night, and he guessed he just did not trust it.

Glen made a wide, shrugging gesture. "We can forget it, if you like, Gary," he said.

"Maybe that would be better."

It was therefore not entirely comfortable for either man that evening. Glen devoted himself rather doggedly to Stephanie while Liz suffered, and Gary began to regret his words to his cousin. He and Glen had once been very close; there wasn't a better fellow anywhere. And if Liz liked him . . .

Stephanie did not think she liked Glen Hollander. Something was insincere about his attentions, she felt, and he was just too tall for her, so that dancing with him was awkward. He did not, however, evince any curiosity about her, which pleased her.

In the powder room, she remarked to Liz, "We really should switch partners. Glen is too tall for me and dancing with him is awful."

"You don't like him?"

"Oh, yes, but I like your Gary better."

"He's not my Gary."

"Well, you know what I mean."

Liz's suffering eased considerably, but she was not very happy, for Glen scarcely looked at her. I wish he'd never come here, she fretted.

Stephanie sensed something wrong. It did not seem a very gay party. And then Glen asked Liz to dance and everything was made plain.

"Gary," Stephanie said with a laugh, "did you see the look on Liz's face? And, Lord, don't they look wonderful together!" She sobered instantly. "What do you think? Is he . . . will he?"

Gary shrugged. "They seem equally smitten, Steph. Not much we can do about it except wait and see. Glen is a nice young fellow."

Stephanie frowned. "You approve? Gary, I know how much you think of Liz. I don't think *I* could bear it if she got hurt."

"Let's give them a chance, Steph. Here they come. Let's dance."

Liz moved in a dream. Glen Hollander had just asked her if she would consider dating him, and had even told her what Gary had said, and how he, Glen, had tried to keep his eyes off her.

They sat alone at the table while Gary and Stephanie danced and danced, and Liz listened while Glen talked earnestly of his plans, of his hopes . . .

The next morning when Liz came begging coffee again, Stephanie teased her a little and saw the tall young woman blush for the first time.

"Sorry," she said.

"That's okay." Liz sat, rubbing the nape of her neck, somehow shy. "I really don't believe it, you know," she said. "Things just don't happen this way."

"What things?"

"Oh, you know, Steph. Meeting someone and right off . . . "

Stephanie was afraid she did know. "Just take it easy, Liz," she said, stern-mouthed. "He may not stay here, you know. And you should get to really know him."

"Oh, I know him already. I know all about him and he knows all about me and — "

"When did all this happen?"

"Oh, at the table, and then he called me this morning and we talked and talked . . . "

Stephanie winced inwardly. Damn men, she thought. And she was afraid for Liz and helpless, for Liz with her trusting nature was going to follow her heart no matter what.

"I guess I'd better get this coffee to Syb," Liz said, standing up and looking touchingly young. "Steph," she added as she moved away, "you do like him, don't you? For me, I mean."

Echoing Mac, Stephanie said, "I like him, I like him."

Liz went off smiling to herself. And Stephanie frowned and did not like Glen Hollander at all!

7

THE romance continued to blossom. Gary Hollander had given the pair his blessing and turned to Stephanie for company, but because she could not agree with him about the rightness of Liz and Glen, she became evasive.

"It's going to work out, Steph," Gary had said. "Glen's going to stay here. I don't know why you seem disapproving."

She had said she neither approved nor disapproved, and in a way it was true. Liz looked so happy and Glen certainly seemed in love. I'm just a darned cynic, she thought. Just because I rushed into marriage with Stan doesn't necessarily mean Glen is like him. Glen Hollander was already a professional man!

Stephanie missed Liz. She saw her

every day at the office, but that was about it. Liz and Glen spent every possible minute together. And springtime lent their romance its own music.

They talked a lot, and of course, Liz confided her interest and affection for her friend. But Glen sensed that Stephanie did not particularly care for him, so he was not enthusiastic.

"Funny she didn't mention being from New York to me," he remarked as they explored Golden Gate Park hand in hand.

"She probably figured Gary told you. Anyway, I don't think she was very happy there. Steph is kind of a loner. The girls at the office grind their teeth because they don't know anything more about her than they did in the beginning."

"Some people are secretive by nature," he said without much interest. At times, he wished Liz would not talk so much about her office friends. He was already a little jealous of this Mac fellow.

"Funny you should say that," Liz

was going on. "Sometimes I get the feeling that Steph has some deep, dark secret." She was laughing. "Our Ginny thinks Steph is *so* mysterious. Ginny's a real cute kid, Glen. One of these days I want you to meet her — all of them."

"I'm satisfied with just you."

"Oh, Glen." Liz leaned against him. "It's still unbelievable, isn't it?"

"I knew, the first minute I saw you."

"Me too. And I was scared silly. Wow, that first night I really suffered. I was so sure you would fall for Steph — "

"She's not my type."

"She'd better not be. But she *is* my best friend. I'd like to see her happy the way I am, Glen . . . "

"She looks happy enough to me."

"I mean really in-love happy."

"Liz, sometimes I think you're too trusting. Isn't there anybody you dislike?"

"Not that I can think of offhand."

Glen felt troubled by the very traits

he most admired in Liz. She was so crazy about Stephanie without knowing anything about her.

"I used to know a Nelson in law school," he remarked presently, since Liz persisted in talking about Stephanie. "He's dead now."

"Steph's husband is dead."

He laughed. "Well, naturally, honey, that's the only way widows happen. Anyway, the Nelson I knew wasn't married, not that I ever heard, anyway."

"Wouldn't you have known?"

"Not necessarily. I didn't know him that well. He was more a friend of a friend of mine."

Liz laughed up at him. "You're a nut," she said, "and I'm hungry."

"You're going to be expensive to keep," he said, affecting a sigh, and Liz came close to giggling. She had never been so happy. They did not speak of marriage in practical terms. Remarks like the one Glen had just made sufficed.

Liz was curiously reticent about her

romance in the office. She had not even confided in Mac; she was waiting until she could flash an engagement ring in his face — and around the office.

But she exuded the radiance that love alone bestows, and Mac noticed and wondered. He remarked to Stephanie one day, "Our Lizzy seems to be in a tizzy. What's up, Steph?"

Stephanie laughed. "She hasn't told you about Glen Hollander?"

"You mean Gary Hollander."

"No, I mean Glen, a cousin of Gary's who just recently came here."

Mac grinned. "You don't say! I've met Gary a few times. Nice chap. If this Glen is anything like him, Liz has my blessings."

"They aren't at all alike. Glen is younger, taller, and very handsome. Liz is just entranced."

"You don't like him?"

"I didn't say that. All I said was, he's not a bit like Gary."

"Okay." He frowned. "Glad you told me, anyway. I'll find out for myself."

"Why does it concern you?" she blurted.

He gave her a quick look, shrugged. "Well now, Steph, that's a good question. I guess it's just that Liz is something special and we're old buddies."

Stephanie was silent, remembering what Liz had told her of his kindness. Not looking at him, she sighed.

"What's the matter?" he asked.

"Matter?"

"That was some sigh."

She laughed thinly. "I didn't realize. It's warm in here, like summer."

"About time for the air conditioning. It is warm." He swiveled his chair around to face her.

"What do you say we throw caution to the winds and go grab us some tall cold drinks?" he said. He stood up and shook his head at her as she hesitated. "Paul's out," he reminded her, "and I'm the boss, remember?"

"Yes, sir," she laughed, then as they left his office, she added as though to herself, "You are a strange man."

"Like me better than you used to?"

"Lots better."

"Me too. I'm getting damn fond of you."

They were laughing as they passed through the reception room. Ginny looked up, all smiles, and thought Stephanie had never looked so pretty.

"Hold down the fort, honey," Mac told her. "Steph and I are playing hookey. May even elope, but keep it under your hat."

"Wish I could go with you."

"You're too young. Try me next year. By then I'll probably be tired of Steph."

Stephanie laughed, shaking her head. "He's a very corrupting influence, Ginny, so watch your step. I go under protest."

Mac gave her a glinting look of appreciation as he held the outer door open for her. "Better and better," he said ambiguously, and watched the coral tints brush her high cheekbones.

Stephanie ducked her head, heart racing. Mac was fun to be with, she thought. She was glad he liked her. She liked him now unreservedly.

Paul Bayliss glimpsed them just as he was about to drive his car down the ramp to the building garage. He did not pause, but his eyes reflected a kind of anger. The image of Stephanie, face lifted in laughter to Mac, had hit him almost like an affront.

Paul did not think of himself as shy, but the incident made him realize how little he had done about his feeling for Stephanie, and he determined to rectify the oversight. But it was odd, he reflected, how when he heard Stephanie's laugh he got the feeling she had deceived him.

He lived a rather sedentary life, his friends the people he and his wife had known. He and Mac did not fraternize socially. He had felt reasonably content, being a creature of habit, until the advent of Stephanie into his life. He had felt oddly sure of her. Now he wondered.

Stephanie had seen Paul. "Let's not be long, Mac. Paul is bound to have scads of work for me."

"Oh forget it, Steph. You're too conscientious. Paul can wait."

"You're the boss," she said, but worriedly.

He gave her a small nudge as they turned in at a restaurant and proceeded to the bar. "Relax," he said. "I never did think that widow woman had any humor, so don't let her creep back in, okay?"

Her laugh was weak, but when they found a table in the gloom, she did relax. "Nothing alcoholic for me," she said. "Just something minty and cold."

He ordered, and she thought he looked pleased with her. "How is your mother?" she asked.

"Fine. She asks about you often, Steph, something about that needlework."

"It's coming along fine. Greta was

115

a big help the night Liz and I were there."

"You ought to go out more often."

"Oh, Mac, I'm not Liz. I can't go barging into someone's house."

"Why not? Mother took a fancy to you and she does get lonely in that damned chair. She used to be very active."

"Yes, I know. You're a strange man," she repeated.

"How so, brown eyes?"

"I don't know." Their drinks arrived and served as a diversion. She did not know she had sighed again until she saw his frown.

"What is it with you, Steph?" he asked bluntly. "Are you carrying the weight of the world on your shoulders, or something? Why so sad?"

"I'm not sad. It's just — " She sought an outlet and found it. "Your laziness is contagious, Mac. You're a very happy person, aren't you?" she surprised herself by adding.

"I have my moments. You know,

Steph, you're a hard person to know. You're young, beautiful, and from all reports don't lack for male companionship, and yet . . . "

"I'm just not the exuberant type, like Liz."

"I think you could be, if you'd let yourself."

She did not like the way the conversation was going. "Do you think we'll get the bid on the housing development?" she asked quickly.

Mac let his breath out on a note of exasperation, then leaned forward. "Look at me, Steph," he said quietly, but with heat, "I'm trying to reach you, trying to learn what makes you tick, because . . . " He sat back, stared at her. "You bother the hell out of me," he ended, puzzled.

"I'm sorry," she said stiffly.

"For what? And don't tighten those pretty lips like that. Pretend we're old friends. My God, Steph, at times you're bitter as gall, and yet when you laugh . . . "

Stephanie suddenly wanted to shout at him. She did not know how her eyes blazed in sudden fury. What do you know? her mind screamed. What do you know about struggling, fighting, just to survive? Easy for you to sit there prying.

"Say it," he ordered, wrung by her look. "For God's sake, Steph, what is it?"

She pushed aside her glass, stood up, and fought for control. "Paul will be wondering," she said at last, coldly. "I really must get back."

His eyes lifted to take her in, then fell away. He got to his feet slowly. "Whatever you say," he said, feeling oddly tired, and he did not speak to her again. In her office, he saw Paul standing in his office doorway. "Looking for Steph?" he asked roughly. "Here she is, safe and sound."

Paul was looking at Stephanie. "So I see," he said distantly. "No, I have no need of her at the moment." And he turned back into his office.

Stephanie made a small sound that was laughter, but so couched in pain that Mac stared at her. Then, rather abruptly, he took her by the arm and half pushed her into his office.

"Whatever it is," he said, "I have a feeling you're suffering more than necessary. I didn't mean to pry, Steph. I'm sorry."

And for the third time a sigh escaped her. The sound seemed intolerable to Mac. In one long stride he had hold of her and before she could turn her face away he was kissing her hard, long, and without joy.

Neither heard the door open nor saw Paul Bayliss look in and quickly withdraw, closing the door soundlessly behind him.

Stephanie felt lost and found in one moment and for a small eternity she did not struggle, but at her first movement of resistance, Mac released her and went rather heavily to sit behind his desk.

"I'm not going to apologize," he

said. "You had it coming to you. I tried — I *did* try to reach you, help you, and now I have no idea why." His eyes widened at her pallor. "Sit down. Do you want a drink of water?"

She shook her head, mouth slack. "I'm — I'm fine. Just let me go now."

Mac was puzzled, concerned, and for once at a loss. He let her go without a word, and something twisted inside him at the odd loneliness of her stiff, careful walk. And then he felt such a sense of loss, he cursed silently. My God, he thought, I think I love her!

Stephanie sat at her desk, hands idle. Her pallor was so deep that Liz let out a little cry at the sight of her. "Steph! Are you ill?"

It was an out. "Feel dizzy . . . "

"Come on, then, I'll take you down to the lounge. Or would you rather go home?" Liz turned as Paul appeared. "Paul, Steph is ill. I think she should go home."

120

He smiled in a small, tight way. "Have someone drive her home, then, Liz. Ask Mac. I have to go out. Let Mac take her."

"Sure." Liz frowned after him. "What's with him? Well, come on, Steph. Or wait, I'll get Mac."

"No." Stephanie got to her feet. "Please, Liz, I feel better already. It's nothing, really. Just the heat."

The office did not seem warm to Liz, but she said, "Okay, but you should lie down."

"All right." Stephanie let herself be led out, glad to leave the office and any sight of Mac, but declined further help when they reached the lounge. "I'll be all right in a little while, Liz. No, I don't want to go home."

Liz left her and headed at once for Mac's office. She did not know, of course, that Stephanie had been out with Mac, but she did know something had to have happened between her and Paul. She had never known him to act so unfeelingly.

She entered Mac's office without knocking. "Say, Mac, Steph got sick." She saw his start. "Oh, nothing serious. Just felt faint, I guess, but she doesn't want to go home." She plopped herself in a chair and regarded him thoughtfully. "Just between you and me, Mac, I think something happened between Steph and Paul. You should have seen the dirty look he gave her — "

"What?"

"There she was, looking like death warmed over, and he just said to let her go home and looked at her as if she were dirt! It really threw me, Mac. You know how he's been about her."

Mac stared away from her. "Where is he now?"

"I don't know. He didn't say. Just went out. I tell you, Mac, something happened! Do you think he proposed and she turned him down?"

"Don't be ridiculous, Liz." Mac was wrestling with guilt, regretting he had let Stephanie go. "Shouldn't you be with Steph?" he growled.

"I'm going back. She says she'll be fine."

"Well," he said carefully, "if she's all right, why fuss? As for Paul, he was probably in a hurry." He got up and moved to his drafting table.

She followed him and stood eying him narrowly. "You didn't see the look he gave her. I don't think she saw it. But, Mac, I just know something happened. You should have heard the way he said, 'Let Mac take her home,' almost sarcastically."

"Liz, you're imagining things." Mac felt as though even his breathing must be careful. "Why don't you go check on her, okay? If she should go home, I'll be glad to drive her."

"Okay." Liz laughed shortly. "But I didn't imagine the look Paul gave her."

"Beat it," he said, trying for humor, and when she was gone he leaned on the table edge and stared unseeingly at the windows. What was it with Paul, jealousy because he had taken Stephanie out for a drink? No, he didn't believe that. Paul wasn't the type.

For a moment, Mac relived the feeling of Stephanie's soft weight in his arms, her nonresisting lips. No one could have seen them. He had closed the door of his office. He was sure of it. Something moved in a corner of his mind. Hadn't there been a sound, a breathing sound?

He straightened. If, by some chance, Paul had come in and seen them, knowing Paul, Mac knew he would have withdrawn quietly. Had that happened? Or was Liz just exaggerating? Whatever, there was nothing he could do about it. It was no crime to kiss a pretty woman. He was just sorry he had let her go.

The big lounge was quiet, unoccupied except for her, and Stephanie lay on her back and studied the ceiling. The old deep-rooted need to survive was at work in her, shock having abated.

Mac had kissed her. Well, so had Jack, on a number of occasions. A kiss is just a kiss. The refrain from a song teased her mind a moment, then she let it go.

All right, she addressed herself. You felt faint, dizzy; June was terribly hot. No crime in that. Must she leave a job simply because one of the bosses kissed her? After all, hadn't Liz once labeled Mac a playboy?

She did not think about Paul at all, for she had been only vaguely conscious of his presence, and Liz had said he had gone out again. She closed her eyes. It'll be all right, she decided. After awhile she'd get up and put on a new face, fix her hair, and return to her desk.

A stray thought opened her eyes. She sat up. Liz would have told Mac where she was — what would he say, do? Would he tell Liz how he had tried to pry into her mind? How she had reacted?

No, her reason answered. No, Mac wouldn't do that. He was sorry he had tormented her; he had not known he was tormenting her. Oh, Mac, she thought, I don't know how to cope with you.

"How do you feel?" Liz was asking. Stephanie lifted her head and nodded. "You look a little better. Mac'll drive you home, if you like."

"No, really, I was just going to wash my face, I'm fine now."

Liz sat down on the edge of the couch. "No hurry. Paul's out and Mac isn't busy. Steph . . ." She looked away, frowning in indecision. "Look," she said, "it's none of my business, but Paul acted so — "

"Paul?"

"Yes, didn't you notice? He acted like he couldn't care less if you dropped dead."

"Liz!" Stephanie stared. "You can't mean that! Why, Paul's the kindest — "

"Then you didn't have some kind of trouble with him?"

"With Paul? Liz, I haven't seen him since early morning, and why would I have trouble?"

Liz stood up. "Okay, if you say so, but I'm not exaggerating, Steph. He really looked daggers at you."

"I can't believe — " Stephanie gave her head a shake. "He surely couldn't have been angry because Mac and I went out for a drink. We weren't gone terribly long."

"You and Mac went for a drink?"

"Yes." Steph did not look at her friend. "It was his idea. We saw Paul driving in, and I told Mac I couldn't be long. I don't think Paul saw us, and he's just not that way."

"Well, forget it. Are you sure you feel okay?"

Stephanie laughed thinly, then stood up and inspected her wrist watch. "Have you had lunch, Liz?"

"Say, maybe that's what you need, some food. Look, I'll go tell the boys I'm going. I'll tell Mac you're okay, then we can go eat. Okay?"

"Yes. Liz, did Paul say when he'd be back?"

"Nope, not a word. I'll be back in a jiffy."

Stephanie could not work up any worry over Paul. He was the most considerate of men. It was Mac who riddled her mind. The little outing for a cold drink had started out in such fun. She had warmed to Mac's approving blue eyes upon her and she had felt so at ease. And then he had just seemed to pounce.

I can't, Mac, she thought meaninglessly. I just can't afford to. I wish I could.

And, oh, I wish you hadn't kissed me — or I hadn't kissed back. I can't afford complications in my life.

"Oh hi," Carmen Foye said, coming in. "Heard you were sick. Are you okay now?"

"Fine, fine."

"Be glad to fix you some lunch."

"Thank you, but no. Liz and I are going out for lunch."

"Okay, but anytime . . . "

Stephanie bit down her lower lip. Carmen was merely being kind. "Thanks," she said again, and left the lounge in search of Liz, feeling depressed. Nothing ever stayed the same for long, and sometimes she got so tired of the struggle.

8

THE afternoon seemed interminable. Stephanie had recovered her poise, but her mind gave her no peace. Paul had not come back; Mac had spoken to her, his eyes constrained yet concerned, before he too left.

"No use you staying around, Steph," he had said. "Want me to drive you home?"

She had declined quickly, saying she had been wanting time to work on the files, and Mac had not insisted. She kept puzzling over Paul's behavior and, like Mac, wondering if Liz had exaggerated. She tried not to think of Mac at all. And the workday ended at last.

"Say, Steph," Liz said. "I'm meeting Glen, but I know he'd be glad to drive you home. You haven't seen his new car yet, anyway."

"No thanks, Liz. I don't feel much like cooking, so I may eat downtown. And I'm fine. Go meet Glen and quit fussing over me."

"You look tired."

"I am, but I'm fine, honestly."

"Well, if you're sure," Liz frowned. "We won't be out too late, Steph, so I'll look in on you later. I know Glen won't mind."

"I'm just going to eat, then go home and go to bed, Liz, so don't bother."

"Well, okay." They were in front of the building, their directions opposite. Liz did not know why she felt uneasy. She glanced at her wrist watch — Glen would be waiting. "Okay," she said again, "but take it easy, will you?"

Stephanie did not eat out. She boarded a cable car, feeling oddly tearful. Liz was such a good, kind-hearted person. Most people were, actually, kind, like Carmen, particularly when there was illness or trouble.

In her apartment, which usually lifted her spirits at just the sight of it,

Stephanie felt oddly averse to being alone.

The rooms felt too close, the thought of food nauseating, so she undressed and took a long luke-warm shower, and lay down on the couch, but not for long. Her mind kept giving her back the early events of the day, Mac's eyes warm, laughing, the kiss . . .

She reached for her portable television set and carried it into the bedroom, which seemed cooler, and she considered air conditioning, rejected the idea as too costly, then unexpectedly, something broke inside her and she stretched face down on the bed in such wild sobbing she frightened herself. She could not seem to stop. She did not know when sleep overcame her, when all that was left of the sobbing were intermittent echoes like hiccoughs.

★ ★ ★

Glen and Liz were having dinner at the Chez Marguerite, and Liz had just finished lecturing him on his extravagance. "Last night Kan's and tonight here," she had ended, rolling her eyes.

"I like taking you nice places."

"You're not by chance rich, are you?"

"Hardly. And when I go into practice for myself, you'll be lucky if I can buy you a hamburger."

"I like hamburgers. We can go Dutch."

"I've got to find an apartment. I can't go on mooching on Gary. I don't suppose there are any vacancies in your building?"

She flushed slightly. "I guess you're really going to stay."

"I told you. One look at you and I knew I was going to like it here — and stay."

"I'll keep my eyes open. There are none in my building right now. Of course . . . " She grinned at him. "I could, maybe, throw Sybil out."

He laughed. "How do you two get along?"

"Oh, all right. She's out a lot, and we have two bedrooms, you know, so we don't fall all over each other. I kind of wish she had taken Steph's single apartment and Steph had moved in with me."

He erased a frown before it could form. "How much rent do you pay for your place?"

She told him, saying, "But you probably just want a bachelor apartment."

"As a matter of fact, no. It's going to take me some time to get a practice going, but one of these days I might want to take a wife, particularly one who abhors extravagance."

Her heart turned over, but she remained outwardly calm. "I suppose I could learn to cook," she said. "I keep planning to have Steph teach me. Say, Glen I don't want to be too late tonight. She was sick at work and I'd like to check on her."

"Dammit," he said.

"What's the matter?"

"Couldn't you tell I was working

up to a proposal?"

"Maybe you shouldn't."

"Why not, for pete's sake?"

"We haven't known each other long enough."

"I know you. You should have been named Kim, little friend of all the world."

"You sound half mad." Liz was enjoying herself, for now that Glen had all but committed himself, she wanted to sit back and savor every minute.

"You are a bit of a patsy, honey."

"Nuts! Just because I think it would be nice to see how Steph is? She'd do the same for me."

"I wonder," he said under his breath.

"Glen! Ye Gods!" she cried. "Don't tell me you're the jealous type — even of my *girlfriends*?"

"Maybe I am. You sure talk about Steph enough. Even spoiled my proposal."

She laughed. "Wow, Glen, you slay me. But that's all right," she added. "I don't think anyone has ever been jealous over me before." Her eyes softened at his expression and she reached and touched his hand. "Glen, I'm only teasing. I'll propose to you, if you like."

He laughed. He was crazy about Liz, just head over heels in love with her, he thought bemusedly, and he really could not pinpoint why. He had thought himself in love before, but Liz was different.

Liz watched him, her heart melting. It really was love at first sight, she thought, and I'd die if I lost him!

On the way home in his new car Liz sat very close and hummed to herself. She felt as though she had known him forever and said so.

"I know the feeling, sweetheart. We really will get married, won't we?"

"As soon as you can afford me." She moved a little apart, turning on the seat. "By the way, you should know, I don't intend to give up my job."

"You really like those people, don't you?"

"Love them. I want you to meet them." She laughed softly. "I really can't even think of marrying you until Mac puts his stamp of approval on you."

He frowned in the dim light from the dashboard and she moved close again alerted by his silence. "Glen?"

"What, Liz?"

"You clam up whenever I mention Steph or any of my friends. You couldn't really be jealous . . . ?"

"I just want nothing else on your mind but me. Do we have to see how Steph is?"

It was wonderful, yet a little frightening. Liz stared ahead, eyes perplexed. "Glen, I haven't said it yet. I'll say it now. I love you."

"Liz, darling — "

"But I wouldn't like it if you couldn't like my friends, and Steph is my best friend."

"All right. What's the matter with her?"

"Oh, the heat got her down. You do

like her, don't you?"

"She's all right. Not my type, I guess."

"She'd better not be!" she repeated.

"I'm going to get you a ring, so we can be engaged. You wouldn't consider marrying me right away?"

"I'd rather be engaged. I've never been engaged." She leaned against him. "Glen, let's not rush things. I'm a wee bit leery of marriage. I'd want mine to last."

Three weeks before, marriage was the last thing in his mind, but now . . . "Ours will last, darling," he said. "I've never felt like this before. Marrying you is all I want."

Liz sighed contentedly, and when he stopped the car near the apartment house, she went into his arms.

Later, hands clasped, they got off the elevator at Liz's floor. For a frozen moment they just stood in shock as unearthly screams resounded all around them.

Then Liz was running. "Steph!" she

shouted. "Steph!"

Right behind her, Glen shouted, "My God, what is it?" And then he took over, pushing Liz aside as he rattled the door knob, then pounded with his fists on the door. Doors opened all down the hall, but this one remained shut.

"Break it down, break it down!" someone suggested.

"Listen, listen," said another, "the screams have stopped."

"Steph! Steph! Steph!" shouted Liz.

Stephanie was in the grip of the nightmare and could not move. She heard the pounding at her front door, but she was completely disoriented.

"Don't, don't, don't, please," she whimpered, and the sound of her own voice wiped the glaze from her eyes. Her heart was thundering and she shuddered, but she knew, knew where she was, what the pounding on the door meant. She heard Liz's voice over those of the others and died a little.

It took her a long time to get off the bed and move across the floor, pulling her robe on as she went. And because it had happened before, she reacted like a robot.

Unlocking the door, she looked out and said, "What is it? Liz, is something wrong?"

A stunned silence followed, and then Liz was pushing in and ordering Glen to send the people away. "My God, Steph, you screamed," she gasped.

Stephanie made a thin sound of laughter. "Liz, I was asleep. I don't know what you're talking about." She looked away to avoid Liz's eyes and saw Glen and gave a start, for he moved close to her and looked down at her almost angrily.

"You were screaming bloody murder a minute ago," he said harshly. "How can you not know? You woke up the whole building!"

Liz put a hand on his arm. "Don't, Glen. Steph, sit down," she said, and sat herself, her legs trembling. "You did scream," she added gently. "You were ill today, Steph. Did you have a dream or something?"

Stephanie fixed her eyes upon Liz now as though for protection, and she willed her mind to function. "I don't know," she said. "Liz, I was dreaming, but I don't remember. I'm sorry, I don't remember anything except — except you screaming. Oh, I'm so confused . . ."

Reaction had set in and suddenly Liz shook so she could not speak, and Glen lifted her to her feet and held her. "For God's sake, honey — " He broke off and almost glared at Stephanie. "She's shook. If you're okay I'm taking her home."

"Yes, do," she said. "I'm fine, fine. Oh, poor Liz. Liz, I'm so sorry!" she cried out, her distress so genuine that Glen looked at her curiously. Why did he have a feeling she had not been sincere moments ago? "Glen, take care of her," she was saying. "Don't bother about me — just take care of Liz."

"I intend to," he said shortly, and he took Liz away, half carrying her and murmuring endearments. Something shouted in his mind at her helplessness. "Liz, darling, I love you, love you . . . "

In her apartment, he put her on the couch and fixed her a drink, holding the glass to her lips. "It's all right, Liz," he begged. "It's all over. Drink, honey — please."

Liz swallowed, coughed, and pushed the glass away. "I'm — I'm okay." She covered her ears with her hands. "Oh, that awful sound, I keep hearing it."

"I know," he said tenderly, and put his arm around her. "Something odd about the whole thing. For a minute there, I could almost have believed it hadn't been she who screamed."

His arms helped. Liz was still shaken, but past shock now. "It was Steph, all right." Her big eyes searched his face for a moment, then she picked up the glass and drained it, grimaced and tried for humor. "I needed that. Oh, Glen, I'm glad you're here. I don't know what I'd have done."

He stroked her hair, his mind back on

Stephanie. "I can't imagine a nightmare making anyone scream like that," he said thoughtfully. Liz shuddered against him and he tightened his hold on her. "Easy does it, baby. I'm going to stay with you until Sybil comes."

"Good. I don't know why it frightened me so," she said, the pupils of her eyes still dilated. "Do you think she's all right?"

"She seemed to be. You were the one who was shook."

Liz stole a look at him. He looked angry and it moved her deeply. Jealous or not, he loved her as no one ever had.

"Are you all right, darling?" he asked.

She nodded, and knew she was, for the last shred of doubt was laid to rest in her mind. It didn't matter that they had known each other such a short time. This was it, for both of them.

"Nerves?" he asked, and she drew apart, her eyes two big question marks. "I was just wondering, Liz, what would make a person scream like that?"

"Steph is the least nervous person I ever knew," she said, "but I suppose it could have been that. She wasn't well at work, you know . . . "

"It keeps bothering me. She didn't look a bit unnerved. I had a funny feeling, Liz, that maybe — maybe, I say — she knew darned well she had screamed."

Liz rather agreed, but loyalty to her friend was strong. "I hope she's all right," she said.

"Do you want me to go see?"

Her heart melted. "No. She was all right, and it's so late. Oh, here's Sybil." She sat away from Glen, but without embarrassment. "Hi Syb, you missed the excitement," she said.

Glen stood, lifting Liz up with him. "I'll go along home now, darling," he said. "Just don't stay up all night talking."

"Oh, I don't expect to sleep. Syb, the most awful thing happened . . . "

Glen left her to her account of

the incident, and not reluctantly. His mind buzzed with darting thoughts and he wanted to be alone to sort them out. Something was not quite right. Something about Stephanie Nelson did not ring true.

What *could* make a grown woman rip apart the silence of the night with such explosive screams? He could not believe just nerves. He did not know what to believe.

"Oh, Gary," he said when he reached his cousin's apartment, "I'm glad you're still up. The damndest thing happened tonight." And he told it from beginning to end, frowning over the rather abortive proposal.

Gary smiled. "Steph could hardly have planned a nightmare to spoil your important evening, Glen," he said. He was more interested in the proposal than the nightmare. "So, you and Liz are going to take the big leap."

"We've lots of planning to do. I'm glad now I delayed coming here and went to Los Angeles. That deal down there was tempting and at least I got the bar exam taken and passed for California, but if I'd stayed I'd not have met Liz."

"It will be quite a venture for you."

"Scares me. I was nothing but a law clerk back East."

"You'll make it. With Liz behind you, you can't miss." Gary looked at his younger cousin with affection. "Guess Steph and I will have to get together to console ourselves."

Glen did not smile. "That screaming really shook Liz up," he said. "Me, too."

"Steph may not have felt well. She's poised enough on the outside, but there's no telling with a person like her. I wouldn't worry about it, though."

Glen shrugged. He did not want to worry about it. And yet, when he went to bed, he could not sleep. He fixed his mind upon Liz, groaning inwardly each time Stephanie's face intruded. Who was she, anyway? And why did tonight's incident seem important? Liz,

Liz, he thought, why have you never asked Stephanie about herself? Wasn't it a bit strange that Stephanie did not confide in Liz, who was such a loyal, trusting soul?

Nelson, he pondered, Nelson. Even the name bothered him, although there was nothing uncommon about it. He had known Nelsons before, hadn't he? Of course! He'd mentioned it to Liz —

When was it Stan Nelson died?

Glen sat up, heart hammering. Oh no, he thought. He was letting his imagination run away with him just because tonight he had seen Liz unnerved. And he was afraid his nature was a bit suspicious.

Nelson, Nelson . . . What had Stephanie's husband's first name been? Nelson. The name droned in his mind as sleep overcame him.

And, waking, it continued to haunt him.

9

MAC bent his head over the drafting table, his face averted from Liz, who still lingered, having been wished the best and kissed because she looked so happy. She had told him the dénouement of the night before.

"Ye Gods, Mac, it scared the wits out of me," she said expansively, the memory now brushed with a sort of excitement and the shock half-forgotten. "I don't know what I'd have done if Glen hadn't been there. He's wonderful, Mac."

"So you've said a dozen times," Mac said against the something in his chest that threatened to squeeze the breath out of him. Liz's too-graphic description of screams that had splintered the night had ripped open an old wound, and an old sickness was upon him. He did not realize how grim his face was as he added, "I'm busy as hell, Liz. Happy for you and all that, but — "

She frowned. "Okay. I suppose I shouldn't have gone on and on like that about Steph. I really just came in to tell you about Glen and me."

"I know. It's okay, honey. Just busy."

She nodded and left, eased of mind, but Mac let his weight fall half across the table as he stared back across the years to himself, a boy not quite fifteen, to a summer day with the family up at the lake. Just the family — Dad, Mother, himself, and the twins, Beth and Bob. Bob.

They were so close, those two, he remembered, as only twins can be. He, four years younger, had always felt odd man out, jealous and competitive where Bob was concerned. And always darkly proud because even at that age he was as tall as Bob and stronger.

But I loved him, Mac thought. And no one ever blamed me, not even

Beth, who was brokenhearted. They called it shock because I saw Bob drown, but it was more than that, and only Mother knew what made me come screaming out of nightmares for months afterward. And Mother had healed, sustained, and brought him through the trauma without permanent damage.

It had never occurred to anyone that young Alex could have reached his big brother in time to save him, and even then Alex himself had not been sure, but if he could have reached Bob . . .

Guilt. Mac knuckled his eyes and groaned, inwardly, painfully. He had been swimming about, showing off for Mother and Beth on the shore, and he had seen how neither was looking at him, but at Bob in a rowboat, fishing. It had angered him, and he had turned to look, just in time to see the boat capsize and Bob disappear. He had just stood there treading water for a small eternity before he moved outward, swimming toward the spot and hearing Beth's screams for help.

If he had tried harder, if he had not wasted those precious minutes, would Bob be alive today?

No, his adult mind told him. When Bob's body was brought to shore it was evident at once that the boat had struck his head in capsizing, probably killed him instantly. Even if he had reached him quickly, it would have been too late.

Mac moved back to his desk, took a bottle from a bottom drawer and raised it to his lips in a long swallow. Long, long ago his mother had absolved him of guilt. And he was not guilty, not of Bob's death, but of the jealousy, of the secret contempt for an older, bookish, and less strong brother. He had wanted to be first in everyone's regard, and everyone looked at Bob with admiration. And Beth and Bob had always had their twin secrets, while he . . .

Mac put the bottle away, reached for his light-weight jacket, and lumbered out of his office. Stephanie was not at her desk.

She looked quite unchanged to Paul as he listened to her read back what he had dictated. He had had time to consider and evaluate the kiss he had witnessed and, while it had altered his opinion of Stephanie in part, he knew Mac too well to hold her completely responsible.

He did not, however, regard Stephanie as a delicate flower now. It was obvious that she no longer grieved for her dead husband. He himself was just now emerging from a long bereavement. Somewhere inside himself Paul sighed.

"Well, that sounds all right, Stephanie," he said when she sat silent, looking at him. "Let it go at that."

Stephanie wondered why his look this morning was touched with sadness. Had he received bad news of some kind yesterday? Liz had said he had rushed away in a great hurry.

"Will that be all then, Paul?" she asked, not rising.

"Yes — and no. Have you seen anything of Mrs. MacArthur lately?"

"No, not since the evening Liz and I went out there."

"How is the needlepoint progressing?"

"I haven't been working on it much lately." She felt something behind his casual words that she could not pinpoint. "I've been pretty busy," she added, feeling oddly guilty.

"I suppose living so close to Liz," he began, then frowned, not wanting to sound critical. "Liz leads a pretty active social life, I understand."

Stephanie laughed briefly. "I'm teaching her to cook and she's very funny about it. She's a wonderful person and a good friend." She thought of Liz's tact in not harping on the nightmare and her own affected indifference.

"If you're free this evening, Stephanie, I've been thinking about calling on Mrs. MacArthur," Paul said, smiling.

"I'm sorry, I'm not free," she said, both glad and sorry that it was so; glad because the talk about her and Paul seemed to have died down and she did not want it revived, and sorry because he seemed sad, lonely.

"Well, perhaps some other time." His eyes had cooled, and after she left he sat quietly, wondering what had made him suggest an evening with her. His feeling for her died hard, he supposed. And, too, he could not help worrying about her where Mac was concerned. Mac was not the marrying kind, as everyone knew.

Stephanie looked at the note Mac had scrawled to apprise her of his absence. His handwriting was much like his personality, big, strong, and decisive. Without thought, she folded the note and put it in her pocketbook. She felt curiously restless.

Liz was not meeting Glen for lunch for once, so she and Stephanie went together to the coffee shop. She was feeling a little guilty about discussing

Stephanie's nightmare with Mac and was hoping he had not mentioned it to her.

"You feel okay today?"

"Oh yes, fine. Liz, I think you must have misunderstood Paul yesterday. I think he must have been just in a hurry. He's certainly the same as ever today. Even invited me to go see Mrs. MacArthur with him this evening."

"Are you going?"

"No. I told him I was busy."

"Oh. Look, Steph, I know you like him. I mean, if you really do, it's nobody's business."

"Liz, I admire him tremendously. But I could never be really interested in him now."

"Now? Why now?"

Stephanie looked away, then laughed. "Now or ever," she said quickly, and realized she had been thinking about Mac. "I'll stick to Jack, if you don't mind, my romantic friend."

Liz grinned, satisfied. "You know,

Steph," she said, "I'm kind of glad about last night. I don't mean that you had a nightmare, but afterward, Glen was so wonderful. It made me very sure about him. It did something — brought us closer, or killed my last doubt. Now, if you don't want to talk about it, just say so."

"I'm glad it helped. I don't remember anything about it."

"Good." Liz's eyes glowed softly. "Glen really was wonderful. He made me feel like a kid, so protected, and all that. It felt good."

"You're a hopeless case, I'm afraid."

"It's funny about love, this real kind," Liz said dreamy-eyed. "It makes me want everyone to be happy, too, and makes me sort of — of clearer-eyed, about other people, you know? Take Mac, for instance. To me he's always been happy-go-lucky, a fun guy, but today when I really looked at him I could see I was wrong. He looked downright unhappy or something. Of course, he might just have been in one of his moods or had a big fight with Tina . . . ″

Stephanie was silent a moment, then asked, "Liz, have you ever seen Tina Marshall?"

"Oh, sure. She used to come around the office a lot to pick him up, but he put a stop to that."

"I suppose she's very beautiful?"

"Yeah, she's beautiful, all right. That woman has everything, looks, money — and Mac." Liz sighed expansively. "Oh well, if it's what he wants, it's okay by me. As I said, I want everybody to be happy. I never could quite see those two, though."

"Why not?"

Liz shrugged. "Too much alike, maybe. Both great catches, as it were, but I've never felt that Mac was really in love with her. To be really in love changes everything. One of these days, Steph, you'll fall in love again and you won't be lonely anymore. I was lonely without knowing it."

Stephanie felt a wave of affection sweep over her. "I'm happy for you, Liz," she said. "I hope it lasts for you. You deserve to be happy."

"Oh, I will!" Liz smiled widely, but her mind had seemed to click like a verification of past wonderings: happiness in marriage had not lasted for Stephanie. It explained much about her, Liz felt. Who wanted to dwell upon old miseries?

"Is Glen picking you up after work?" Stephanie asked as they made their way back to the office.

"Yes. Want a ride home?"

"No thanks, Jack is picking me up. He thinks it's terrible I've never had the thrill of the Crookedest Street. If I live through it, he's promised me dinner at Omar Khayyam's."

"He takes you to nice places. Glen is the same, but we're cutting out all that now and saving our pennies." Liz laughed happily. "We're just going to a movie tonight."

Back at her desk, Stephanie sighed.

Liz's talk of love had saddened her. She felt she might very well have forfeited the right to her own happiness. She was not *un*happy. She had been very lucky: in her job, Liz, and someone like Jack Ripley to take her out of herself for hours at a time.

And she was deeply grateful that the nightmare had brought no repercussions. Anyone could have a nightmare, and screaming could always be denied as long as she lived alone.

"Did you see Mac?"

Stephanie came out of her thoughts to find Paul standing in front of her desk. "Mac? No. He went out — won't be back today."

"He came back a while ago, Stephanie. I told him you were out to lunch. He seemed to have something on his mind."

"Oh?" She was aware of something intent in Paul's eyes. "I wonder what, Paul," she said quickly. "I finished the financial statement he wanted first thing this morning. I got the figures from Accounting and I'm sure I copied them correctly."

His eyes remained intent. "I don't think it was, ah, business," he said, and turned away. "No doubt he'll call you."

She regarded his closed door with a bewilderment that extended to the man himself. His eyes had seemed almost suspicious, she thought, and his behaviour had been decidedly odd.

She shook off unanswerable thoughts. She was just overly sensitive. Paul could not know that Mac had kissed her. Mac himself seemed to have forgotten it.

What had he wanted?

Paul Bayliss was wondering the same thing. Mac had come in looking for Stephanie, looking oddly harried, then had gone out again without a word of explanation. Paul could not get the picture of Stephanie out of his mind as he had found her moments before, sitting idle and looking almost desolate.

A thread of anger against Mac ran

through his mind. If Mac was toying with Stephanie's affections . . . Still, she was no innocent girl!

For a moment, Paul almost smiled. In a way, he reflected, it was as well he had witnessed the two of them kissing. It had banished forever the thought that Stephanie in any way was like Elaine. It was not Stephanie's fault, he added in fairness. She had never given him any reason to believe she could *care* for him. And, perhaps, she did not care for Mac, either.

The thought bothered Paul. It put her in a light he did not care to dwell upon. He was suddenly glad he had never tried to date her, glad she had refused his invitation to call upon Mac's mother this evening.

She's not the right one, he decided, but he felt a sense of loss. Stephanie, he thought. Lovely name. Lovely girl. But not for him.

He smiled at her warmly as he left for the day, and bewildered Stephanie all over again. She wanted to laugh;

161

yet she felt like crying. Things seemed to be changing again, her sweetly won plateau giving way under her feet.

She bent her head as though under a weight, and into her mind stole the memory of Glen Hollander the night before, and the angry way he had looked at her and seemed to see through her.

Stephanie felt threatened. She told herself it was ridiculous, she was just tired; Glen had been upset over Liz. But something had gone out of the day. Mac, she thought. It had all begun with his kiss. For a long, lost moment, she had felt right in his arms. If he had not let her go. If he had not said, "You had that coming to you."

And yet he was right to let me go. I have no place in his world, she decided firmly.

10

MAC drove aimlessly. He was glad now that Stephanie had been out to lunch. The impulse to reach her, face her, make her speak out, had been a bad one.

He thought off and on now about Tina Marshall, who could no longer matter. Funny about women, he mused. For weeks Tina had been accusing him of having some other woman in his life, and he had mocked her for a fool. Now he admitted that she had been right.

For a long time, perhaps from the beginning, when she had irritated him constantly, Stephanie Nelson had been at the back of his mind.

I love her, Mac thought. But what of her? I've never been able to believe in her as a sorrowing widow. I've fought believing anything good about her right along.

He sighed to find himself in front of his mother's house and turning in. He didn't even have a new book to give her or a handy excuse for an afternoon visit. Oh well, he thought, she's always glad to see me.

He did not notice his sister's car until he was at the front door, which Beth opened before he could escape.

"Aha," she laughed. "So this is how you run your company! What brings you home at this hour, little brother?"

He laughed shortly and looked down at her with inward regret. He did not feel in the mood to exchange glib talk.

"Hi, Beth," he said, going ahead of her to the living room. "How is Thorn these days?"

"Thorn is working, working hard, which is more than I can say for — "

"Alex!" his mother cried out softly. "What a nice surprise. Have you had lunch?"

"Yes," he lied. "I was out this way on business." He flicked his sister a

164

sardonic look. "Thought I'd surprise you, Mother, by *not* having a mystery book for you!"

His mother laughed, but her eyes took him in obliquely and she felt a sudden pang. Something was wrong, she knew instinctively, but nothing that could be shared with Beth.

"Alex, guess what? I saw your new secretary downtown with Liz Peterson," Beth began.

"She's hardly new, Beth."

"Well, whatever. I didn't get a chance to talk to them, but I did get a good look at Mrs. Nelson. Not bad. Not bad at all. I hear Paul is badly smitten."

"Oh, dear," their mother said. "Beth, you know we said no such thing. Alex, sit down, dear . . . "

Beth was not easily put off. "Mother says you brought your secretary here for lunch one day, Alex. Just what is the score? And did you know our mother insists she has seen Stephanie Nelson somewhere before?"

"Beth — " He broke off and sat down

heavily, his eyes taking in his sister with a trace of pain. His memories of her twin, of her bitter loss, made him gentle with her now. "I don't know why you are so interested in Stephanie Nelson. She's a good secretary and a pretty nice woman. You'd have to ask Paul how he feels about her."

Beth was not unfeeling. She had been teasing Alex since he was born, it seemed. Now she looked at him thoughtfully. "I saw Tina the other day," she said. "Is that what has you looking a bit ragged around the edges?"

He blew out his breath, but the subject of Tina was safe ground, so he was not dismayed. "Since when have you and Tina become chummy?" he asked with some of his usual glibness with his sister.

"Actually, she called me and we had lunch. Must say I was surprised. She was so tense, not like herself. Seems to think your devotion is waning, or something . . . "

Mac frowned. It did not sound like

proud Tina Marshall. "Are you sure you didn't call her?" he asked. "You are a terrible snoop, you know."

"Now, Alex," his mother said.

"It's all right, Mother," Beth laughed. "Tina *did* call me and I admit I was curious. But she was the one doing the snooping." She sat down near her brother. "Have you found a new love, brother mine? You certainly have Tina going in circles."

Mac stood up and gave his sister a token punch. "Ask me no questions, I'll tell you no lies, sister mine," he said lightly, but for a moment his eyes brooded upon her. Poor Beth, he thought. "You're looking very well these days," he added in altered tones. "What's new in the yachting set?"

"You must bring Tina to the club soon," she said, her mind diverted. "Thorn wants to get up a party and go sailing."

"I'll think about it." Mac looked down at his mother, smiled, and was suddenly glad of Beth's presence. He might have been tempted otherwise to speak of Stephanie and the nightmare. "I should be getting back to work," he told her.

"Very well, dear," she smiled in return, then made a mistake. "Do tell Stephanie we're anxious to see how her needlepoint is coming along."

"Okay." Mac moved outward, but Beth was too quick for him, and a little taken aback.

"I say, Alex, no offense meant. I mean, if it is this Stephanie Nelson who has taken Tina's place in your — "

"How would you like to mind your own business for once?" Mac glared at her in sudden rage, and rushed away without even a word for his mother. And Beth stared after him, a soft flush touching her lovely face.

"Mama," she said, "why didn't you tell me?"

"Tell you what? That you are a most tactless young woman?" Althea MacArthur spoke in anger because she, too, was a little taken aback, and considerably worried.

Greta Hansen moved into the breach, as was her wont. "I see no reason to jump to conclusions," she said sensibly. "Beth, your mother has become very fond of Stephanie, as she is fond of Liz, I expect Alex did not like being put in a false position."

"What position? Good Lord, I couldn't care less about his love life."

"Beth, I don't like that kind of talk," her mother reproached her, anger abating. "It does seem you'd outgrow your need to tease."

"Since when is *he* so sensitive?" Beth did not like being in the wrong and did not think she deserved reproach. "Honestly, Mother," she said in a hurt tone, "Tina did call me and she did intimate that all was not well between her and Alex. It seems she is right, and about time Alex admitted it. I've a good mind to let her know about this Stephanie."

"Don't be crude," her mother said. "Alex is quite able to handle his own affairs. Beth, dear," she added, "I know you don't mean to be unkind. Your brother does not seem too happy."

Beth was silent a moment, then said, "Sorry, Mama. I suppose it all means that both Alex and Paul are smitten by their secretary. She looked very attractive when I saw her, with Liz, but she can't hold a candle to Tina. What *is* so fascinating about her that even you are — "

"She is a very nice young woman, Beth, and as Greta said, we have no reason to jump to conclusions. I think we'd best forget it."

"It must be tough," Beth mused, not unkindly. "I mean, if it is true, Mother. Our Alex is not one to take defeat lying down. Have you seen Paul lately?"

"Oh, Beth, for heaven's sake."

"All right, all right." Beth reached for her pocketbook and gloves, moved to depart, and then turned. "Mother, do you really feel you have seen this Stephanie before?"

"Stop calling her *this* Stephanie, but,

yes, I do feel I have. And I'm probably wrong."

Beth frowned. "You need to get out more," she said with genuine concern. "It's not good for you just sitting about imagining things. Why not let me drive you somewhere tomorrow, Mother? Just the other day Miss Cunningham was asking about you. Not that she gets out much, herself."

"Miss Cunningham?" For a moment, her mother stared across at Greta, then quickly recovered from her brief shock. "Well now, I'm glad to hear she is getting out at all, Beth. How is she?"

"Looks the same as she did to me when I was a mere child."

"Yes, well, I'm glad you mentioned her, Beth. And yes, perhaps you're right. I'll give her a call and perhaps you can drive me there one day."

"Do that, Mother. You know I'll be glad to take you anywhere, anytime."

"I know, dear. You're a good girl."

"Don't forget to call her. Or shall I?"

"I'll do it, later today, and let you know."

"Good. It's what you need, to get out more."

After Beth was gone, her mother became oddly agitated. "Greta," she said, "is our old family album still in the library?"

"I think so. Thea, what is it?"

"Probably nothing. Just something I thought of. Help me turn this blasted chair around, will you?"

Greta obeyed, her thoughts busy. "It's something about Miss Cunningham, isn't it? But what?"

"Greta, dear, how long have you been with us?"

"Twenty — no, nearly twenty-one years. Thea, what on earth is it?"

"You'd not remember her."

"Miss Cunningham? Thea, for heaven's sake!"

"Alicia Cunningham had a younger sister. Her name was Madge. You'd not remember her because she left, oh, twenty-five years ago at least. Maybe more." They had reached the library. "I just want to look at some old snaps and photos, Greta. I could be wrong . . ."

Greta found the big faded album. Looking worried, she put it in the other's lap, saying, "You haven't looked so excited in ages, Thea."

"I am excited." She turned pages, peering at the array of pictures. "You see, dear," she explained, "when Beth mentioned Miss Cunningham, it triggered something in my mind. Madge was very much younger than Alicia, but she was at least thirty when she went off with that man — " Her finger pounced on a faded photograph. "Yes," she said, "yes. Look, Greta, this is Madge Cunningham, taken when she was around twenty. Who does she remind you of?"

Greta had pulled up a chair and now took the album. "My goodness," she said. "Yes, I see the resemblance. How very odd!" She laughed shortly, relievedly. "Well, now your little mystery is solved. Now you know why you *thought* you had seen Stephanie before!"

Althea was silent, frowning, and Greta regarded her with new concern, for now the little woman seemed to have paled. "Now what new scheme are you plotting?"

"Nothing. Nothing. It couldn't be. And yet . . . " Closing her eyes briefly, Althea shook her head. "I'm getting addlepated, Greta. I don't feel right about it. That old photo, it must be thirty years old, and I feel as though I've seen Stephanie recently, at least not years ago."

"I think you'd better rest awhile," Greta said, and closed the album. "That imagination of yours is working overtime. Beth is right. You should get out more — and the weather so fine. You read altogether too many of those mysteries."

Althea laughed thinly. She had not relinquished the album and there was a brightness in her eyes Greta deplored.

"There's not that much resemblance," Greta grumbled as they moved back to the living room.

"You're right, of course," the other woman agreed when she was settled. "You might hand me the phone, dear." And responding to Greta's frown, "Now, I did promise not to forget to call Miss Cunningham."

Greta sighed when the call was completed. "She's a stiff-necked old woman, Thea," she said. "Couldn't you have thought of someone else to visit?"

"Greta, Alicia Cunningham is a proud old woman. Not that she's that old. Not as old as I." She gave her faithful housekeeper a long, affectionate look. "Alicia never married, you know. And it did look as though Madge would follow suit. They lived together in that big old house, as prim and proper as you please. Then quite suddenly, shockingly to Alicia, Madge eloped with a strange man. She was over thirty, poor thing, and I suppose her outlook was bleak. Alicia was the dominant one, more like a mother to Madge than a sister. I liked Madge. In a plain sort of way, she was very good-looking. Lovely eyes . . . "

"Where did she go?"

"East, somewhere. She wrote Alicia, but Alicia was hurt, angry and proud, and I guess after a while, Madge just didn't write. It's been over a quarter of a century, Greta, a long time. And sad that Alicia could not forgive . . . "

"Who was the man?"

Althea frowned in recall. "Madge and my brother's oldest girl were friends. Agatha might know. Too bad Agatha chose this particular time to go abroad. Agatha is in her fifties now, as Madge would be, if she's alive."

"Your niece never married either, but she strikes me as a natural spinster. Well, Thea, I'll make you a cup of tea."

"Yes, do that, dear." And alone, Althea MacArthur opened the album again. The eyes were really very much like Stephanie's, she mused. And there could have been a child . . . She sighed, wondering if the restrictions of her days had affected her mind.

Still, she thought, according to Liz Peterson, nothing was known about Stephanie before she came to San Francisco. There did not seem to be any family.

The thought took hold. She could be wrong, Althea MacArthur conceded, but ever since she had met Stephanie, something about her had riddled her mind.

I wonder what her maiden name was. I do think I shall mention Madge to Alicia when I call. It's been so many years and Alicia is growing old.

Oh, dear, she sighed, perhaps I am bored, and yet so much seems to be happening. Alex and his troubled mind — clearly to do with Stephanie. And the problem of Paul and Stephanie. And then dear Liz . . .

Well, that was a happy note. Liz was in love and headed for the altar.

She was going to bring her young man soon.

"Tea," said Greta.

"Ah, good. Greta, don't you think we should have Liz and her young man to dinner soon?"

"Yes, I do," said Greta, glad her old friend had gotten over her fancies.

11

GLEN HOLLANDER'S height, strong build, and good looks belied an unsure nature. His mother had been very strong and until her death he had relied upon her judgment and common sense. His life had been easy and comfortable; his mother had not been possessive. It had been her wish to see him married and settled before she died, and it seemed now to Glen that she would have approved Liz.

In the days following Stephanie Nelson's screaming nightmare, Glen fought for some of the common sense that had been his mother's and was Liz's. His mind swung pendulously over the thought of Stephanie; he did not wish to think about her or consider what might be true about her. Yet, whenever Liz mentioned her, which was often, he felt afraid.

His fear led him to an act he was to regret later. With Liz working, he had time on his hands, and it seemed everywhere he turned an empty telephone booth stood beckoning him. At last, he stepped into one and placed a long-distance call to New York.

Glen had spoken the truth when he said he had not known Stanley Nelson well, but he remembered him. Stan had not been the type one easily overlooked and Glen had envied him his air of self-confidence.

Pete Bagley, a close friend who had graduated from law school with Glen, had been the one who knew Stan Nelson personally, and had continued to see him and his crowd when Stan dropped out of school.

Glen had run into Pete shortly before leaving the East and had been surprised to learn from him that Stan had died under peculiar circumstances. He had not felt any great interest because he had not been in the city at the time of the death and had hardly been aware of anything but his own grief over the loss of his mother.

When he emerged from the telephone booth his face was rather pale. Stan Nelson's wife had been Stephanie, no doubt of it, and she had been accused of murdering him. No one knew what had happened to her afterward; she just disappeared, and according to Pete Bagley, regardless of the verdict that freed her, many still believed her guilty.

Glen did not know what to do.

He wondered how he could avoid telling Liz or whether he should, and how she would take it if he did. He was not strong enough to remain silent, however, and on a night when Liz was talking happily about her friend he felt the truth boil in his mind.

"She's crazy about Omar Khayyam's," Liz was saying. "That's where she and Jack are tonight. I'm glad for her, Glen, glad I introduced her to him. I swear, she's seen more of San Francisco than I have already."

"I wish you'd let me take you nice places," Glen said. They had been to a movie and the thought of Stephanie enjoying the best places moved him to anger. "I can take you to Omar Khayyam's or any other of those places, Liz."

"You know we agreed to save our money, and I don't care where we go or what we do, so long as we're together. You know that."

"I know, but it's not as if I were broke."

She knew to a penny how unbroke he was, but her mind was practical. "Look, darling," she said, "I've been thinking and thinking, and maybe we're crazy to wait. I don't really care about an engagement ring. I'd rather be married."

His heart leaped, but he said, "I care about an engagement ring and you shall have one. And, Liz, honey, the office space I looked at is in a good location and there's an apartment I saw the other day . . . " He smiled, teasing.

"I thought you didn't believe we knew each other well enough yet."

"Oh, I was just being feminine. I figure with your savings and what I make — and you'll soon have trillions of clients — and we can manage *if* we watch our pennies." Her mind soared. "We can just have a small wedding in a chapel, Glen. Mac will give me away and you'll have Gary for your best man, and I'll have Steph!"

"Liz . . . " The mention of Stephanie cooled his enthusiasm. If Liz knew, would she still want Stephanie for a matron of honor? Could he stand the idea? Did he have a right *not* to tell Liz?

Liz was watching him and sensing a change. She drew in her breath. Was she being too pushy, coming on too strong? But this was Glen and he did want to marry her and she'd felt he did need a little push. What if she were wrong?

"Glen," she said. "I'm sorry."

He turned on the seat of the car.

"*Sorry*? Liz, darling — you've changed your mind? Liz, sorry about what?"

For a second relief closed her eyes, then she laughed and went into his arms. "Nothing, nothing," she cried out softly. "Just so happy it scares me."

Glen held her, eyes troubled. At times, she almost seemed to read his mind.

"Liz," he said suddenly, "why don't we just elope?"

She drew away, eyes wide. "Elope? But why? Oh, Glen, no. I want a wedding and all my friends there and yours . . ."

"I don't have any here but Gary."

"Still, I wouldn't like eloping." She peered into his face. "What is it, Glen? I know there's something wrong. Please, darling — ?"

He could not meet her eyes. For a desperate moment he thought he'd just say nothing, forget it, and then he heard himself say, "Liz, honey, I know how you feel about Steph. And I *don't* dislike her. You have to believe that!"

Liz stared at him. "What about Steph?"

"Don't look at me like that. Oh, Liz, do you remember me telling you about a Nelson I knew in law school?"

Liz frowned at his tone as much as the words. "I think I remember, yes," she said. "What about him?"

"His name was Stanley Nelson. He was Steph's husband."

"You knew Steph's husband and you haven't said a word about it until now? Why, Glen? I don't get it."

"Listen, then. I didn't know him well. He was Pete Bagley's friend. I didn't know until the other day that he was Steph's husband."

"The other day?"

"Yes. I was out of the city at the time it happened and then I bumped into Pete just before I left New York. It was Pete who told me Stan was dead and Steph was arrested — "

"*What*? Arrested? When was this?"

Glen felt a touch of anger even as

he said, "Now, don't go getting mad. Hear me out. I always felt there was something odd about Stephanie and how not even you knew anything about her. And you might as well know, Liz. She was driving the car. She pushed Stan out of it and ran over him."

Liz's mouth hung open, and for a moment Glen was frightened. "Look, she was freed. I called Pete the other day and he told me."

"You called him — you called New York?"

"I felt we should know."

"*We* should know?" Liz laughed shrilly, then in a movement too swift for him to prevent, she was out of his car and running into the apartment building.

He caught up with her at the elevator, which she tried to prevent him entering. "Now, wait!" he panted. "Be fair, Liz! I only did it for you! You're so damned trusting."

"And you're so damned small!" she flared, then in sudden misery, she let him enter the elevator, and added as it ascended, "Why did you have to do it? Why couldn't you let it alone?"

He felt as though he were fighting for his life. "Try to understand," he begged. "Why, Liz, even now, people back there don't believe she was innocent. And, honey, be reasonable, you must have wondered about her yourself."

"So, I wondered, but I didn't go snooping, prying, like you." She hurried ahead at her floor, blinking back tears. If it had been anyone but Glen, she grieved. Why couldn't he have let it alone? Of course Steph was innocent! Steph wouldn't hurt a fly!

"No," she said as Glen tried to enter the apartment. "Go away, Glen. I don't want to talk to you. I don't want to see you again — *ever*!"

He took a step back, eyes shocked, and in a heartsick moment, Liz looked at him. So tall, so handsome, and so very young-looking. Big dumb ox, she thought. "All right, come in," for she could not bear to lose him no matter how in the wrong he was.

"Oh, Glen," she said again, "why couldn't you let it alone?"

He sat down heavily, looking at her with eyes filled with guilt, but said, "Isn't it better to know? The truth is always best, Liz . . . "

"I didn't need the truth," she said bitterly. "I accept Steph as she is. We're friends. And now I have to work with her, live down the hall from her, see her, talk to her, knowing this . . . "

"Might it not be better to tell her you know?"

"You don't know anything, do you?" she cried. "I could never do that to her. And she'd have told me, herself, sometime, I know she would! I don't believe a word of it, anyway."

"Pete knew Stan. He even met Steph a couple of times. If she really was innocent, how come she couldn't even tell you about it? God knows you've been more than honest with her!"

If she really was innocent, Liz thought. If she really *were* innocent. She argued the verb to keep her mind from considering the sentence. Until that moment her sense of outrage had been against Glen, and she still felt sick about it, but now she had to look at it straight on. Stephanie had been arrested, accused of killing her husband. No one would lie about a thing like that. But not guilty, Liz added quickly. She had been judged not guilty.

"Liz . . . " Glen, watching her and wondering nervously what she was thinking behind her closed eyes, leaned forward. "Liz, honey . . . "

"Glen, tell me from the beginning," she said, and looked at him quickly as he moved to rise. "No, stay where you are! I can't think if you . . . Stay where you are."

He felt encouraged, but her hurt look made him curse himself inwardly. "From what Pete told me on the phone, the case never came to trial," he began, and almost smiled at the swift change in her. "There was a hearing, of course — and Steph had been arrested."

Her face resumed its bitter look. "She had to be in jail? She was innocent and she had to be in jail? Why?"

"Well, honey, bail is rarely allowed in a homicide," he said gently. "Pete wasn't at the hearing; he had to work, but he's going to try to get me a copy of the transcript. Liz, honey, witnesses swore she pushed her husband from the car."

Liz folded her arms, studied the pattern of the carpet. "This Pete," she said at length. "You say he knew Steph. But you didn't, Glen . . . "

"I didn't even know Stan was married. Pete said he didn't either until after Stan flunked out of law school."

"He flunked out? Glen, tell me about this Stan Nelson. How come Pete didn't know he was married?"

"Well, Stan was one of those

personality guys. Girls crazy about him and all that. He was a year behind Pete and me at law school, but he was the kind of guy you noticed. Even after he flunked out his close friends were from school."

"What did he look like?"

"Oh, terrific looking. Almost as tall as I am, but blondish. Real good-looking guy and, like I said, lots of personality and very popular."

"Mmm. Sounds like a chaser to me."

Glen tried to laugh. "I guess he didn't lack for girls. Pete said he was really surprised when he met Steph. It was long after Stan dropped out. Pete said none of the gang knew Stan was married and Steph was quite a shock."

"How do you mean?"

"Just not somebody you'd expect Stan to choose, and I guess she wasn't very likeable. Anyway, Pete didn't like her and he said Stan's folks couldn't stand her."

Liz closed her eyes. "What about Steph's folks?"

"She has none as far as Pete knows. She had a couple of character witnesses at the hearing, but no family showed up. The judge pretty much dismissed the case, Liz, but Pete says people still believe it was no accident."

"People . . . who are the people?"

"Well, Stan's family and his friends . . . "

"What happened?"

Glen stood up, paced back and forth, and at last stood in front of her. "There was a party. Pete was there. He said Steph was a party pooper and kept nagging at Stan to stop drinking. She wasn't much of a partygoer, I guess. Anyway, she got him to leave the party early and they had a big scene about who would drive, she saying he was too drunk and embarrassed Stan, I guess, in front of his friends."

"I don't think I'd have liked him."

Glen shrugged, and continued. "Well, she drove, and they were arguing. A witness in the car behind testified that she saw Steph push Stan out of the car . . . and she did run over him, Liz. He died before they could get him to a hospital."

"She didn't mean to," Liz said stubbornly, "and she was let go. Nothing will make me believe it wasn't an accident." She got to her feet and regarded Glen with sorrowing eyes. "I wish you hadn't — I wish you'd let it alone."

He felt tired, used up, guilty. "Do you want me to go?" he asked.

Her eyes took in the height of him. "Why did you, Glen?"

"I told you. Something about her bothered me, and you're so damned trusting. And, too, Liz, I couldn't forget how she screamed. It was so unlike her . . . "

"Yes." Liz shivered in remembrance. "But it must have been awful for her. Didn't anybody stand up for her?"

"Someone must have. She was freed." Glen shook his head. "I'm sorry, Liz, but if it hadn't been me it would have been somebody else."

"What do you mean?"

"I mean, just any time someone could see her and recognize her. Maybe I should have let it alone, but I didn't. It was bound to be known sometime."

Liz granted this possibility, but it did not ease the pain.

The look on her face tortured his mind. "Liz, Liz, I am sorry. I do love you . . . "

She lifted her face and, slowly, touched his face with her hand. "Promise me one thing?"

"Anything."

"Leave it alone now. Just you and I are to know and no one else, all right? I'm sorry I know, sorry you pried, but there's nothing to be done about it now. I just don't want . . . anything . . . changed."

"All right, we'll just forget it."

Mockery came and went in her big eyes. *Forget it?* He had sowed the seeds of doubt in her mind despite her loyalty to Steph, and *he* said forget it?

"I'm tired," she said. "I know it's not terribly late, but I am, Glen. Okay?"

He bent and kissed her, relieved that she permitted it. "Am I forgiven?"

A sadness touched her as she nodded. There he stood with all his fine education, his law degree, smart as a whip in his profession, and yet so immature.

And here I am, she added when she was alone, just old Liz Peterson, who never even finished high school, and yet I feel older than Glen tonight and smarter, too, in ways in which he might never be.

So all right, she shrugged. So he's no Sir Galahad, no knight in shining armor. So he's not perfect. Who is?

But she cried for a long time before she slept that night.

12

THE Crookedest Street, as it is called, is one way with S-curves down steep Lombard Street from Hyde to Leavenworth Street, on Russian Hill. Stephanie had found it thrilling and scary, and had experienced the exciting ride for the second time.

And for the second time, she sat with Jack Ripley in the superb dining room at Omar Khayyam's with its original murals from *The Rubaiyat*, and sighed with delight over her thick, juicy, charcoal-broiled steak.

"You are spoiling me, Jack."

"My pleasure, sweets. It stirs up my jaded appetites to watch you have fun."

She liked him tremendously, chiefly because he made no demands, but also because through him she was tasting and glimpsing a strata of life unknown before. With Jack, she cast all worry aside and just enjoyed. At times she had an odd feeling of belonging when she looked about at the well-dressed, sophisticated diners, a feeling she mocked and called wishful thinking.

Jack remarked, "I could almost consider another plunge into matrimony when I look at you, Stephanie."

She laughed. "I'm glad you added that *almost*."

"Yes, I'm cautious that way. One of many things I like about you is that I feel so safe with you. I'm very eligible, you know, and considered quite a catch."

"I'm sure," she murmured. "I see you as the perennial bachelor, Jack, and I the perennial widow."

"We're so intelligent," he agreed, and again she laughed. He was the perfect escort and so self-absorbed it never occurred to him to probe beyond the surface of anyone's life. Simply perfect for her, Stephanie had come to believe.

At the table not far away, Mac and Tina Marshall were not enjoying a farewell dinner. She had taken his decision well, with haughty self-pride, but inwardly she was furious. He still denied there was any other woman, but she did not believe it. There had to be.

In the silence that had fallen between them, Stephanie's laugh, so unmistakable to Mac, quite suddenly reached him. His head swung about and Tina's eyes followed the movement. Mac was staring at the laughing Stephanie all too revealingly.

And Tina said, "So I was right." When he did not answer or remove his eyes from Stephanie, she stood up, snatched up her wrap from the back of her chair, and flashed marvelously dark eyes at him in contempt. "Goodbye, Mr. MacArthur," she said haughtily. "You look like a sick calf."

Stephanie had turned to look at the tall, beautiful, and elegant woman who walked as though she owned the earth.

She wondered aloud who she was.

"Oh, don't you know?" Jack asked. "That is society's pet, the one and only Tina Marshall. *And* looking ready to bite nails."

Stephanie stiffened, looked away quickly from the striding woman, and then felt as though she were drowning in the penetrating blue of Mac's eyes.

Jack was still watching Tina Marshall's exit. "Has everything, that girl," he remarked, and frowned faintly. "She and MacArthur are an old item. I wonder why she's alone? Oh, there's MacArthur — " He broke off and looked at Stephanie, then laughed. "Say, that's right, you work for Bayliss and MacArthur. Stephanie, anything wrong?"

"Don't be silly," she snapped, and he stared. But she could not consider him; she was fighting a queer panic, because Mac was on his feet now and approaching.

And then, he was passing their table with nothing but one hot, angry look at her, so that she felt slapped, and Jack laughed again. "That's odd," he said with interest. "Either he was too intent on catching up with Tina or he deliberately snubbed you, sweets."

"Oh, be quiet!" Nerves jumping, Stephanie was staring after Mac.

"I say." Almost impossible to offend, Jack spoke with malicious glee. "Well, well, so that's how the wind blows. Why didn't you tell me? My dear Stephanie, you *are* aiming high, but I should warn you — "

"Jack, will you be quiet?" Her composure returning slowly, Stephanie suddenly felt his shallowness like an affront. "You don't know what you're talking about," she added coldly.

"Oh, don't I? My dear girl, I'm completely intrigued. There have been rumors that all was not well with the town's favorite twosome, but to think . . . And you are his secretary or something, aren't you? It's precious! Did they quarrel over you, do you think? *He* looked ready to kill."

"Jack," she said, stern-lipped, "I want to go home."

"I do believe I've struck a nerve!" he said with excitement, then, "Of course, of course, sweets — "

"And don't call me sweets" she snapped, at which he merely looked more delighted, and he quite cheerfully saw her home, even kissing her lightly in parting.

Stephanie, engrossed in the workings of her own being, hardly saw him at all. The long moment of staring into Mac's eyes *and* his brief, furious glance as he rushed by the table juggled in her mind, but she could define neither.

She felt lonely, deeply and hurtingly lonely in the privacy of her apartment, and she knew it must always be so now. She had seen the beautiful Tina Marshall and knew herself as nothing beside her.

Mac, Mac, she silently wept. If only you had never kissed me.

★ ★ ★

Mac had followed Tina and caught up with her just as she was getting in a cab. He had been summarily dismissed and was now driving about aimlessly. He felt a little crazed.

He did not call it jealousy, but his reaction to seeing Stephanie with another man seemed to have no other name. Tina did not matter. Tina was encased in her pride and would survive. She would remember how he had followed her and begged her to wait, not rush off.

But Stephanie was a different matter. How lovely she had looked, dark eyes shining into his for that moment. Why had he rushed by like that? All he had wanted to do was snatch her away from her escort and tell her . . .

He groaned inwardly. For the first time in his life he was at a loss. Stephanie laughing with that man, she had no need for him, Alex MacArthur. The whole thing was insane.

He hardly realized where he was until he saw the lights burning in his mother's house. He parked, glancing at his wrist watch. It was not late, but it was late for his mother.

Greta Hansen opened the front door to him before he could find his key. "Well, thank goodness!" she said. "Maybe you can do something with her." And she hurried away.

"Greta!" he shouted, following. "What's she doing in the library at this hour?" He felt a touch of fear. "Greta, answer me!" And she turned, shrugged and waved him inward.

"See for yourself. She's been going through old issues of the New York *Daily News* ever since Beth brought us home from Miss Cunningham's."

Althea MacArthur looked up brightly as Mac descended upon her. "Oh, Alex, how nice! Greta is being tiresome and no help at all. Now you can help."

He looked at the strewn papers, then at his mother's slightly flushed face. "What in God's name are you doing?" he demanded.

Greta spoke up in disgust. "At first, Alex, she said she just wanted to clean out that closet — and at this hour!"

"Well, it is a fire hazard with all these old papers. Oh, Alex, sit down. I'm getting a kink in my neck. And don't look at me as if I'd lost my mind. You remember, don't you, when Thorn and Beth gave me the subscription to the *Daily News*? It ran out last December."

Mac pulled a chair close. "All right, Mother," he said carefully. "Just what are you looking for?"

"How clever of you, dear." She gave Greta an arch look. "*She* fussed so, I decided not to tell her. And, anyway, I can't be sure. And yet I've felt all along there was something I should remember, and tonight at Miss Cunningham's I did!"

"Old Miss Cunningham. Is she still alive?"

"Don't be facetious, Alex."

Greta made a tut-tutting sound.

"Thea, you ought not to be up at this hour. Alex, she got it into her head that Stephanie resembles a sister of Miss Cunningham who eloped with some strange man years ago."

"Show him the album, Greta."

Greta did so with reluctance. "Well," she went on, "you know your mother when she gets a bee in her bonnet. Nothing would do but we'd go see Miss Cunningham — fat lot of good it did us!"

"Hush, Greta. I saw no reason to rouse any hope in the poor soul. She's mellowed these past few years, but she never was the same after Madge left — and she's so proud."

Mac was looking at the photo Greta pointed out, and he made a low, strangled sound of laughter. "Mother, you're impossible."

"You don't see the resemblance?"

"Not really. A superficial likeness, maybe."

She looked disappointed, but said

with a note of satisfaction, "I did not, of course, say anything to Alicia about our Stephanie. And, anyway," she added, "just out of nowhere, I remembered those papers."

Mac, who had been mulling over the "our Stephanie," was diverted. "What about these papers, Mother?"

"Somewhere, in one of them, is the face of Stephanie, or someone very like. I'm probably wrong about everything, Alex, but I shall not rest tonight until I find it."

He looked at her with a touch of fear, then shook it off. She was far from senile. She loved mysteries and murders and what-have-you, but she was not senile.

"Well, let's start looking," he said resignedly, thinking it was a queer night altogether.

"What do you know about Stephanie?" his mother asked as they began.

"Not a damned thing."

"So Liz says, too. Seemed odd, too, when they are such great friends. What

206

was Stephanie's husband's name, first name?"

He shook his head. "Personnel might know."

"One hates to snoop."

Greta laughed. "You should have heard her at Miss Cunningham's, Alex. You never heard such pointed reminiscing."

Mac grinned at his mother, but she ignored them both, and he suddenly felt a great reluctance for the task she had set them to. He tossed aside the paper he had been searching through and stood up, and then slowly bent to look at it where it had opened. And aloud he said, "Oh, God."

His mother's head came up. "You've found it! Alex, what is it?"

For a moment he resented her. "Here, take a look! Hope you're satisfied." And he moved away, his face grim.

"Oh dear," his mother said behind him, and Greta drew in her breath as she, too, examined the paper, the small picture of Stephanie and the words: *Wife Held in Husband's Death*.

Althea MacArthur's face looked rather gray, but she kept her wits about her. "This is November. Greta, dear, find the December issues. There must be more than this."

"Mother." Mac turned, eyes angry. "Leave it alone. Steph is free. I'm sure she was found innocent. We have no right to — " He broke off.

She bowed her head slightly at his tone. "I remembered the picture only, Alex, not anything about . . . Alex, we'll do whatever you say."

"Do nothing." He was suffering almost intolerably, but his tone was hard, even.

"What are you going to do, dear?"

"Go home and go to bed."

"Alex, I mean about — "

"Nothing. Nothing. I'd say she's been hurt enough."

Greta had continued to look through the papers and now sighed. "Nothing in any issue after that one, Thea," she said. "And I think Alex is right."

"Oh, I wish I'd never remembered at all!"

"Mother, you meant no harm. Steph must never know." His face worked, and under his breath, he muttered, "Guilt. I knew it had to be . . . "

"What, dear?"

"Nothing. Go to bed, Mother." He bent and tore the picture and item from the paper and put it in his wallet. "I'll keep this. You *try* to forget it and — " He wiped at his face to control it. "For God's sake, never let Steph feel there's anything . . . "

"We promise, Alex. Greta, I'm tired."

"Good night, Mother, Greta," said Mac and lumbered out of the house.

"Oh, Greta," his mother said, "it hurt him. He cares about her. Don't you think? He looked so . . . "

"I'm past thinking tonight, Thea."

"Yes, yes, enough for tonight."

Mac drove homeward, his thoughts on fire. Steph, Steph, my dearest, so that's it . . . and you so alone. Alone with some aftermath of guilt that brings you screaming out of nightmares. How well I know — if only I could tell you.

And tonight he had walked right past her with a look of fury. Mac groaned aloud. But there was hope for her, wasn't there? That lovely laugh of hers, those shining brown eyes. I love her, he thought in near panic, and I'm helpless to help her.

13

IF Mac went about with a pre-occupied air, Liz Peterson did no less. Her nature was too open to bear the burden of secret knowledge easily. It did not help that she would not let Glen speak of it at all. And so, at times she found herself staring at Stephanie and wanting to shout: tell me, tell me!

Liz did not doubt Stephanie's innocence, but it was not possible for her to forget and not from time to time to wonder. It had been a terrible ordeal to experience, Liz told herself, and anyone would want to forget it, put it behind her. But they were friends, weren't they? Couldn't Steph tell *her*?

Stephanie was not without her own preoccupations, for now to sit beside Mac's desk as he dictated was both joy and agony, and she could not look him in the eye. Life had altered again subtly, and now her old will to survive was attenuated. In spirit, she felt tired.

Paul Bayliss, having relinquished any thought of Stephanie as a part of his private life, from time to time felt an odd concern about her. He had heard of the rift between Mac and Tina Marshall, but it was not his nature to pry; he wished he did not have this feeling that Stephanie had figured in the break-up. Certainly, he had nothing to substantiate such a feeling.

Paul did, however, and without real motive, decide to call upon Mac's mother, and he extended a second invitation to Stephanie to accompany him.

"Thank you, but no, Paul," she said, eyes averted, and gave no explanation, which made him both self-conscious and a little resentful.

"As you wish," he said with an air of pride. Well, he thought, watching her as she left his office, if there is anything going on between her and Mac, she might feel shy of visiting his mother, but it does seem odd. Somehow, he could not imagine Stephanie engaged in an office affair. Mac, himself, looked upon such things with disfavor.

Paul considered the male magnetism that Mac possessed and a new thought took hold. Of course, he reflected, it was clear enough: Stephanie had fallen for Mac, and Mac, as usual, was discouraging any hope of permanency. Poor Stephanie, Paul thought. Now if she could only have cared for *him* . . .

Althea MacArthur was delighted with Paul's visit, her keen old eyes quick to assess him. Not changed at all, she decided. Not changed as Alex was changed by love for Stephanie. Still, she had to be sure.

"Paul, my dear, Beth was asking about you the other day. Seems she hasn't seen you for some time, and you know Beth . . . " She gave a small laugh. "She has decided it is time you married again, and assumes that is what makes you so elusive."

He laughed, shaking his head. "I suppose it's natural," he said. "Beth, being so happily married to Thornton, wants us all married, but I'm afraid in this case, she's wrong."

"You're still a young man, Paul. I'm sure it is what Elaine would have wanted for you."

"Yes," he nodded, "but as yet I've found no one to take her place, if anyone ever could."

The little woman hid her satisfaction well. "You mustn't be too choosy," she said. "I'm sure there are many lovely young women in this city who would make you happy, and, perhaps, give you the family you've always wanted."

"Well, bring them on," he said cheerfully. "I admit I find life more and more unsatisfactory, and I know it is what Elaine would want for me."

"Then you'll find someone suitable, I'm sure." Since it was not in him to dissemble, Althea was now without doubt where he was concerned.

Paul felt better for the visit. She was an easy woman to talk to and he was sure of her affection.

"I suppose you've given up trying to marry off that son of yours," he remarked jokingly.

"Now, Paul, I wouldn't *try* to marry off either of you. I must say, though, I'm glad it is not to be Tina Marshall for him. I suppose you know they no longer are seeing each other?"

He nodded, smiled. "I suppose he has found someone who pleases him more."

She looked at him sharply, briefly. "I would not know about that," she said. "Alex keeps his personal life very personal. I'd like to see him married and settled, of course, but he seems satisfied with the status quo."

The visit ended with both feeling the better for it. Althea was relieved that Paul was not hankering after Stephanie; Paul was relieved that Stephanie did not seem to figure in Mac's plans.

And Stephanie went her way quietly,

sadly, and wondered how long she could bear to work so near to yet so distant from Mac. She saw little of Liz outside of the office, was not comfortable dating Jack Ripley anymore, and out of sheer loneliness went to a movie now and then with Gary. But more and more she withdrew into herself and tried to revive the old sense of rightness in being alone.

Returning from lunch alone, Stephanie sat a little apart from the others in the company lounge and pretended interest in a book she carried. But the conversation around her was impossible to ignore.

"Everybody figures it's on account of his breaking up with that Marshall woman."

"She sure is beautiful. Well, it serves Mac right. He couldn't expect her to wait around forever, could he?"

"I wonder if he knew ahead of time?"

"I bet he didn't. Let me see that part of the paper again, will you?"

"I don't care whether he's a duke or a prince," Carmen was saying jealously. "Nobody can tell me she isn't just marrying him because she couldn't get Mac."

"Gosh, she's really beautiful. Hey, Liz, you and Mac are so chummy . . . What do you think?"

"I don't think, I know. Mac just isn't the marrying kind and old Tina finally got it through her head, so she's gotten herself engaged to this Lord What's-His-Name. It won't do her any good. It won't make Mac rush back to her."

"When are you getting married, Liz?"

"Just any day now." Liz regarded the diamond on her left hand lovingly, and for a moment let her eyes take in Stephanie. "Don't be surprised if I just don't show up to work one day. I was telling Mac just yesterday, Glen and I may elope."

Stephanie looked up, saw how Liz's eyes fell away from her, and sensed now what she had only vaguely felt before, a change in Liz. It gave her a cold feeling in the pit of her stomach. But why? she wondered. What have I done to offend her?

When they left the lounge she said, "Liz, you didn't mean it, did you? About eloping?"

"We've talked about it."

"But, Liz, it doesn't seem . . . I always see you married in a church and a reception with all your friends drinking champagne, and I your — "

"We haven't decided," Liz said. "What do you think of that Tina going to marry an English lord?"

"I didn't know, not until just now. She's very beautiful."

"You saw the picture in the paper?" Glad of the subject change, Liz was more herself. "Between you and me, Stephanie, I never thought she had a chance even if she is beautiful. That picture doesn't do her justice. She's one of the few beautiful women in the world, I bet."

"I know."

"Oh? Have you seen her?"

"Yes, the last time I went to Omar Khayyam's with Jack."

"Yeah? How is Jack?"

"All right, I guess. I don't see him much anymore."

Liz stole a look at her. Stephanie looked sad. Oh God, Liz thought, I wonder if she has noticed a difference in me. I try, but what I know keeps getting in the way.

"If you're not tied up, let's have a Coke this afternoon, okay?"

"Sure, Liz. Paul's going out and Mac . . . I don't think he'll want me."

"Old Mac sure is walking around like a thunder cloud, but nothing will make me believe it's on account of Tina Marshall."

"He's pretty busy."

"Well, see you around three, Steph."

At her desk, Stephanie considered Liz's remark about Mac. She, herself, was so self-conscious around him now that it took all her will power to appear unmoved in his presence. She had not looked directly at him for some time. Was there something wrong? She did not like to think of him other than carefree and bantering.

She did look at him, if obliquely, when he joined her and Liz in the coffee shop that afternoon. Liz, as usual, did all the talking, and he listened absently. Stephanie thought there were lines in his face she had not noticed before.

"It's a nice apartment," Liz was saying. "Not as nice as we hope to have some day, but it will do."

"When is the big day?"

"Not sure yet."

"Well, let me know. I get to give the bride away, remember."

Stephanie wondered why Liz did not mention eloping. She hoped she would not; it had something to do with her own elopement long ago and the marriage that had ended so tragically. She wanted very much for Liz to be happy and have a real wedding. She wanted Mac to be happy, too.

"Why so quiet?" Mac asked her.

She managed a laugh. "I didn't know it was my turn."

It was a trite old joke, but the other two laughed rather too much and Stephanie had a curious feeling, she felt as though they watched her from a distance, with both scorn and pity. Back at her desk, she found a resolve forming in her mind: as soon as Liz was married and settled, she would resign, quit her job and move — perhaps out of the city altogether.

The building had pretty much emptied at five o'clock when Mac emerged from his office. He was glad of new work that kept him busy for long hours and distracted him somewhat from the thought of Stephanie. For the first time that he could remember, Mac felt lonely.

In the reception room he paused at the sight of Liz at Ginny's desk. "What's this, Liz?"

"Hi, Mac, nothing. Just waiting for

Glen to call or get here. How are you?"

The question made him look at her more closely. She seemed nervous, and it occurred to Mac that he had half detected a change in her recently without giving it attention. "Anything wrong, honey?" he asked, and saw the start she gave.

"Not a thing," she said. "Look, Mac, I'll put the board up before I leave."

"Naturally," he said and sat on the edge of the desk. "This is your old Dutch Uncle Mac, Liz. Better tell me what's making you so nervous."

"Don't be silly." She looked everywhere but at him and began to talk very fast. "Glen figured he'd be late picking me up. He had a lot to do today, an appointment with the Bar Association about his license and signing the lease on his office space and we're going to go see — "

"Busy, busy, eh?"

For a moment, Liz's eyes lifted to him. If I could only tell him, she was thinking. He liked Stephanie a lot now, and hadn't he always been able to still *her* troubled waters? But how could she tell him it was Glen who had . . .

"Liz," Mac was saying gently, "I know it's a big step. Not having second thoughts, are you?"

"No! Oh no, it's not Glen . . . " She looked away. "It's not anything, just something about Steph I know — " She gasped in relief as the switchboard buzzed for attention. "Bayliss and Mac — who? Oh, Gary. Yes, this is Liz. No, not yet. A telegram? Well, I'll tell him and — " Her eyes found Glen beyond the glass front door. "Hang on, Gary, he's here. Mac, will you let Glen in?"

Mac obliged and made himself known to Glen, inwardly regretting the interruption. Liz was in some kind of trouble that concerned Steph . . .

"Take the call on that phone over there," Liz directed Glen and looked relieved by his presence. She did not look at Mac, who was lingering, but kept her eyes on Glen and openly listened to his conversation with his cousin. And watching, she felt her nerve ends jump, for Glen spoke briefly and his face had paled.

She stared at him questioningly when he replaced the receiver, but he merely moved toward her, saying, "About ready to go, honey?"

"Glen," she began, then, conscious of Mac, turned away. "Be with you in a minute."

Mac did not know why he did not leave. Liz's nervousness bothered him and now Glen, too, seemed uneasy and anxious to be gone.

"Look," Mac said bluntly, "if there's anything wrong, anything I can do . . . Liz, I'd really like to talk to you . . . "

"But we're late already!" she cried, and having secured the switchboard for the night, she took Glen's arm and steered him outward. "See you tomorrow, Mac!" And they were gone, and he was back in his office, pacing, and fighting the thought of Steph, who, too easily, could fill his mind.

Yet he could not dismiss the thought that Liz was worried, unhappy. Had he sensed something estranged between Liz and Steph today, or was he just too imaginative? Liz talking too fast and Steph's face closed, secret as it had been in the beginning. Mac swore again, but could not dislodge the two together in his mind.

Did Liz know what he knew about Steph? Had Steph told her and Liz turned from her? No, no, Liz would never do that!

The through line that kept his telephone open was intact, but Mac replaced the receiver he had picked up to call Stephanie. Then his phone rang and he snatched it up as if it were hot.

"MacArthur," he barked. "Who? Oh yes, I remember you, Gary. No, they've gone. Catch them? I'm afraid not. Anything I can do? They seemed nervous about something."

Gary Hollander considered Mac,

knew him for a good friend of Liz's, and decided to confide in him. He had, he said, just received a very puzzling call from New York, from one Peter Bagley, the same who had sent a wire earlier.

"I don't know what it's all about," Gary said, "but this Bagley fellow sounded urgent. Said he *had* to talk to Glen right away. Do you have any idea where they went?"

"I was here when you called before. The wire seemed to upset Glen. Mind telling me what was in it?"

"I guess not. Didn't make sense to me. Just said for Glen to tell Steph that Maude was on her way. Then this phone call. Bagley sounded frantic. I gave him Liz's number. I could hardly understand him, but he sure wanted to get hold of Glen."

"Did he mention the name Maude on the phone?"

"No. What do you make of it?"

"I don't know, but I'll find Glen. It sounds important, long distance like that."

"That's what I figured."

"All right, Gary, thanks," Mac said and hung up abruptly, his heart beating too fast. Steph, he thought. Something to do with Steph. Swiftly, he dialed her number and heard it ring and ring without answer. He slammed the receiver down and left.

In Liz's apartment Glen listened with shocked eyes to the voice of Pete Bagley in New York, and Liz sat close, straining to hear.

"What is it?" she cried out when he hung up. Glen took hold of her and she felt him tremble. "Glen!"

"Oh God," he said, "it's all my fault. Liz, Pete went to see Stan Nelson's sister, Maude, and like a fool he told her that Steph is here. And now he's frantic. He says this Maude is crazy. Liz, Liz, she's on her way here — *she could be here already*!"

"Here? What — what does it mean?"

"Pete says he found the lawyer who defended Steph and got a different slant on things. Pete says everyone

227

was wrong about Steph and after he saw Maude, he knew the judge had been right."

"The judge?"

"At the hearing. The judge said the case should never have been and threw it out of court, and this Maude had to be removed bodily . . . and she's crazy, Liz, and after Steph to — "

Liz moved swiftly, left, and returned. "Not home yet. Glen, we must stay, get hold of Steph before — Sh! Listen! The elevator. No, not Steph, too heavy a tread."

"Just the same. My God, Liz, if anything happens to her . . . " Glen went and flung open the door, peered out, then stopped short, an arm holding Liz back.

There were two figures down the hall at Stephanie's door — and one was Stephanie.

"Hey!" Glen shouted, moving out.

Stephanie's head turned along with that of a tall, heavy-set woman behind her, then in an instant the woman had pushed her inward. Glen and Liz heard the slam of the door and the key being turned in the lock.

"Glen!" Liz cried. "That woman had a knife!"

"I know. Stand back, Liz. No time for the police. Stand away, darling, I'm going to break down that door."

Liz stood transfixed in fear for him for a moment before she swung about. "Mac!" she shouted as he came striding down the hall. "Quick, quick, a woman has Steph in there — with a knife!"

Mac brushed her aside, eyes on Glen. "All right," he said softly. "All right, Glen. Together . . . *now*!"

14

MAUDE NELSON was close to six feet in height and solidly built. Her face, never attractive, was fearsome in the ugly venom it held now as she tilted Stephanie's head back by the hair and put the knife to her throat.

It had not occurred to Stephanie to struggle after the first shock waves of fear struck her when she stepped onto the elevator on the ground floor and felt herself pushed forward and glimpsed Stan's sister. Nor had it occurred to her to lie when Maude demanded the correct floor number. She recognized madness and the knife had been at her back.

Now, in her immaculate kitchen, on a straight chair, she sat pinned down by a heavy knee across her thighs and muted by a bandana-sized handkerchief stuffed in her mouth. And she knew the end would not come swiftly or mercifully.

"Scum, scum," Maude was snarling, "I knew I'd find out some day and make you pay. You killed my baby brother and now I'm going to kill you."

In some remote part of her being, Steph was resigned. Just get it over, her eyes and mind begged the woman. And numbly, she knew it was no use.

Liz's face loomed in her mind. Don't try, she silently beseeched. Don't let Glen try. I'm so tired, and it doesn't matter now . . . now you'll know Liz, and Mac will know . . . and I'll be better off dead.

Maude did not even hear the first time the front door shuddered with the weight of the men outside. Stephanie heard and closed her eyes in fear for Liz. Behind the gag her vocal cords strained, begging Maude to finish it — end it and be satisfied — and don't hurt Liz!

The door splintered, cracked, and the whole apartment seemed to shake as it gave, crashing inward. Maude's head lifted, but the knife at Stephanie's throat remained steady and Maude's voice did not falter as it poured out abuse.

Mac was first in, waving Glen and Liz back as he glimpsed what was happening through the open kitchen door. The danger to Stephanie held him motionless for a moment, then he moved cautiously forward, the carpeting silencing his tread.

"My beautiful, beautiful boy." Maude was half crooning now. "You killed him. You took my darling and made his life hell, then you killed him . . . and you killed my father . . . and now my mother's dead . . . and you must die. Feel the sharp edge, nameless one? You dared — dared — you without a name dared to marry my darling . . . " The knife pressed, and now both Mac and Glen saw how Stephanie's legs jerked.

Liz, trying to see and turning wild

with terror when she did see, began to scream and scream. The sound pierced the room and echoed, and Maude straightened, turned . . . And in a split second Mac was upon her, an iron grip on the wrist that held the knife, and Glen was lunging forward.

Maude fought with deranged strength as both men sought to restrain her and wrest the knife from her. She kicked out at Stephanie, who doubled up.

Mac shouted, "Shut up, Liz, and get Steph out of here!"

Liz shut up fast and rushed to her friend. Trying to avoid the struggling other three, she pulled Stephanie free and dragged her into the living room, yanking at the gag.

"Get out, both of you!" Mac yelled, and Stephanie's eyes came to life. Leaning against Liz, she swallowed hard, gasped.

"Don't hurt her, please," she managed.

The words brought Liz out of shock. "Don't hurt *her*? Steph, for God's sake, she was going to kill you!" Liz all but pushed Stephanie out of the apartment.

The two men had wrestled the big woman to the floor, where she still fought them, but when Glen held her down by the shoulders, Mac moved quickly to step on the wrist that held the knife. He stepped hard, and bent to pick it up when with a yell of pain Maude let it go. But still she fought, and at last, Glen's fist connected with her jaw, and she was still.

"See if Steph's hurt," Mac panted.

Glen caught up with the girls at Liz's door and she bit down hard on her lower lip at the blood on his face. "Glen — "

"Is she hurt?"

"I don't know. There's blood . . . but, no, she can walk . . . "

"Take care of her," he said, and went back to Mac.

Liz got Stephanie inside and onto a chair, diverted from Glen's face by the look of her. "It's all right, Steph," she pleaded. "Glen and Mac will take care of — of everything. Oh, Steph, don't look like that — it's all over!"

Stephanie shuddered, closed her eyes, and moaned, and Liz made a soft cry of distress, but she had herself in control. She made her friend swallow a straight shot of bourbon and took one herself, then rushed to get a damp cloth and bathe Stephanie's throat, talking all the while.

"I never doubted you, Steph. I knew you were innocent. It's not deep — more a scratch than a cut. That woman — she's insane — and she came so close. And it was an accident, I know it was, about your husband . . . and she's just insane."

For an eon of pain the earth spun around in Stephanie's head. Liz *knew* . . . and if Liz knew . . . "Oh my God," she sobbed suddenly, but she pushed aside the cold cloth against her throat and sat forward. "Liz, you know?"

About to nod, Liz sprang up. "Wait," she said, and ran to the door. She opened it a crack in time to see Glen and Mac, Maude held firmly between them, about to enter the elevator. For a second, Mac looked back and saw her.

"Is Steph all right?" At Liz's nod, he added. "Stay with her. We're taking this one to my doctor."

Stephanie had stumbled after Liz and she saw Mac's grim face before the elevator door closed. She swayed, close to fainting. Liz led her to a couch and made her lie down. "It's all right, Steph. Oh, thank God Mac came. But Glen would have managed . . . "

"Liz — Liz — "

"It's all right, I tell you! Listen, Steph, it's over, done, and you're safe. I always knew you were innocent. Oh, Steph — " And unexpectedly, Liz began to cry.

Stephanie roused herself, put her arms about her weeping friend, and did not notice the tears that wet her own cheeks. And at last, she asked, "Liz, dear, Liz, how did you — when did you — know?"

"Crazy time to cry, when it's all over," Liz said, sitting apart, her thoughts darting to Glen, and her loyalty sharp. "Don't worry about that now, Steph. Wait till the men come back. I'm going to have another drink. Want one?"

Stephanie shook her head, the thought of Mac flooding her mind. She *had* to know!

"Liz, please," she said. "Does Mac know?"

Liz frowned. She dropped ice cubes in a tall glass, and looked out at Stephanie from the kitchen. "I don't see how he could," she said reflectively at length. "I don't even know how he happened to be here." She carried her drink back to the couch. "Anyway, don't worry about it. Glen and I will never tell. And that woman is insane. She'll never bother you again. Just don't worry about anything."

Stephanie closed her eyes. For a moment it did not matter how Liz knew. It was Mac who mattered. Even if he did not know, the past had caught up with her. Mac would have to be told. He had seen Maude try to kill her and he had to have heard why. Stephanie almost wished Maude had succeeded.

"Liz," she said in sudden calm, "I did not love my husband. I was going to leave him. But I never wished him dead. He was drunk and I was angry, disgusted, sick of him, but when he tried to grab the steering wheel I only tried to stop him — he lost his balance . . . I asked him and asked him to have that car door fixed! He fell out . . . He died."

"You don't have to tell me," Liz said with some nervousness. She did not want to have to tell Stephanie how she had learned of the fatal accident. She drained her glass, stood up. "I wonder how long the men will be . . . "

Stephanie lifted a hand to her throat and the distorted face of Maude Nelson loomed in her mind. "They worshipped Stan," she went on dully. "Maude, his

parents . . . He could do no wrong."
She did not seem to notice that Liz
had moved away. "I was not a good
wife. Oh, in the beginning, maybe,
I tried, but he was so . . . And he
knew I didn't know who I was and he
told them, and they hated me more.
I wasn't good enough for Stan, for
their adored one. I was a nobody."
An aborted laugh died in her throat.
"I still don't know who I am and never
shall."

Liz stood quite still in the kitchen
doorway and her big eyes closed as the
voice went on and on, laying bare all
there was to know of her beginnings,
the Smiths, the running away, and
being alone until Stan. And then still
alone.

"He wasn't a bad person. Stan just
wasn't right for me or I for him, but I
never wished him dead. He didn't love
me, but in a crazy sort of way he didn't
want to lose me. Sometimes, I thought
it was his way of getting back at his
folks. He wasn't stupid — he used

them, me — but they had made him that way. I knew it was no good, no good, but I never wanted him dead."

Slowly, Liz returned and took both her hands. "Never mind," she said, "never mind. Both of us, are sort of alike. I always felt it. And now we can be *really* friends, Steph, and put it all behind."

"Oh, Liz, I'm sorry. I should have told you, but I couldn't. I wanted to forget . . . "

"That's all right. After seeing that Maude I don't blame you. Anyone would want to forget her! And you were innocent."

Stephanie's smile was a travesty. "No one is ever completely innocent, Liz."

Hard knuckles rapped at the door and Glen came in, followed by Mac. Liz gave a cry and rushed to Glen, who wore a bandage on his forehead.

"Glen! Darling! Is it bad?" she cried, and clutched at him as though she'd never let him go.

"Not bad, just seven stitches. It's

nothing, Liz." His voice dropped to a whisper. "Nothing to what I deserve," he said for her alone.

Mac had gone straight to Stephanie, who stood up, arms hanging limp at her sides in utter defeat.

"You," he said, "are coming with me."

She made a small mewling sound at the grim anger of his face. Had he come to take her to the police? "I'm ready," she said.

"What's the idea?" Liz wanted to know.

"No idea. You take care of Glen. I'll take care of Steph."

"But, wait a minute — " Liz caught Glen's eyes and stopped, but when Mac had taken Stephanie away, she turned on him clamorously.

Glen put fingers over her lips. "Listen," he said. "He loves her, Liz. Didn't you know?"

Liz looked as though she were going to laugh in disbelief as he removed his fingers, but something in his eyes gave her pause. And she was suddenly remembering how Mac had looked back to ask, "Is Steph all right?"

"Well, I'll be damned."

Glen laughed. "I could use a drink before I tell you what happened."

Over drinks at the kitchen table, he told her, "We didn't have any trouble with her. After she came to — I didn't hit her too hard — she was almost docile. Mac's doctor put her in the hospital for observation, but there's no doubt, Liz, she's insane. When we left her, she was laughing and acting like a kid and talking to her little brother . . ."

"It is kind of sad."

"She'd have killed Steph."

"What will happen to her?"

"She'll get treatment in some mental institution. Liz, did Steph say whether the woman has any relatives?"

"There's nobody now, I guess."

"Nobody to notify?"

"I don't think so. Glen, Steph told me all about herself — everything. It

242

was an accident. She never wanted her husband dead."

Glen covered his face with his hands. "God, when I think how close *she* came to being killed, and all my fault . . . "

"Don't, Glen. Steph will be fine now, and we'll never tell and always be friends." She frowned suddenly. "Does Mac know? Steph asked."

He removed his hands. "That's a funny thing, Liz. He seemed to . . . You didn't tell him?"

"No! You know I wouldn't."

"Well, he knows. I'm sure he does, Liz. Just something about the way he acted."

She was quiet a moment. "I hope he does," she said then. "If he knows and loves her, see? Mac's a terrific guy. He won't let anything hurt her again."

He held her close. "I still feel guilty."

Liz thought of what Stephanie had said. "I guess there's no person in the world who doesn't harbor some guilt about something."

"I love you, Liz. I love you."

"Yes," she said, and laughed softly, "and now we won't elope or just go to City Hall, Glen. We'll have a real wedding. Mac will give me away, Gary will be your best man . . . " Her eyes teased him gently. "And I'll have Steph," she ended.

He nodded. "You're wonderful," he said.

She nodded, satisfied that he thought so. And kissed him to end the talking that could only go in circles now.

15

MAC was driving and talking without haste. He had not stopped talking since he had put Stephanie in his car and driven off, and, curiously, his talk had been all about himself – himself as he had been when not quite fifteen years old.

Stephanie glanced at him from time to time with a strong sense of unreality, but she listened intently, hoping for a clue to what he was talking about. His profile was still grim and somewhat angry, but he apparently had no thought of the police.

Once Mac had determined for himself that Stephanie had sustained no more than scratches on her throat, and had recovered from shock, he had made up his mind to have it out with her.

It had not taken him long to put two and two together back in his office.

Liz and Glen knew something about Stephanie that frightened them; young Hollander was from New York, and he was a lawyer. And a Peter Bagley in New York was frantic to get hold of Glen to warn him. To warn him to warn Steph? Mac knew instinctively that Stephanie was in danger, and that was enough to take him speeding across town to her apartment.

"So, you see," he was saying now, "the mind is a very complicated thing, Steph. It plays tricks on us. And then, of course, there's that depthless storehouse, our subconscious, to make things more complicated. But here's the point, darling, here's the thing to keep us sane. Listen, Steph, there is no such thing as utter guilt or utter innocence . . ."

"Mac," she said, speaking for the first time.

"Yes, Steph."

"Say that again."

He did, his eyes flicking to her as he drove with a quickening of hope. She had to do it herself though, he felt. Her eyes had closed and tears were pushing under her eyelids. He was quiet. He had said all he could say, and now all he could do was wait and hope that the dam of her stricken being would break, and she would talk.

It was not until salt sea air struck at her nostrils that she opened her eyes, sat up straighter on the seat and turned her head toward him. "Mac," she said, "I was guilty of wanting my husband to be what he could never be; I was innocent of ever wishing him dead. And yet, he would not have died that night if I'd been kinder, more tolerant . . . if I had not, in a moment of angry self-righteousness, belittled his manhood and enraged him."

Mac drove slowly until he could park the car facing the sea and the last faint glow of sunset on the horizon. His hands on the steering wheel, he did not look at her or reach for the cigarette he wanted. It was her turn.

"It's not the same, you know," she

was saying. "You were just a boy. I was nineteen when I married Stan and I should have had the strength, the grace, to leave him before I was twenty. I didn't. He didn't want me to. But it was never right between us. I was too proud to admit failure and maybe, just maybe, I liked feeling superior to him, succeeding where he failed, no matter that I did not know who I was."

Mac's blue eyes were still upon the darkening sea, Stephanie's moved nervously and unseeingly. When he reached and took her hand, she seemed not to notice, and her voice went on and on until he could bear no more. She lay against him as his arms went around her, and he let her cry for a long time.

When he was driving again, Stephanie sat a little apart, her mind washed clean of self. "Mac," she said, "what about Maude?"

"She's quiet. Don't worry about her. She'll be well taken care of, I promise you. It's sad, Steph, but she probably was never quite stable. Was she never kind to you?"

"She couldn't be. She loved Stan too much."

"Yes, much too much," he said.

She was quiet a moment, and then, "Mac, you do understand, don't you? Stan was not a bad, mean person. He never meant to hurt anyone. He didn't even know when he did."

"I understand." They rode in silence for a few miles, and then Mac said thoughtfully, "Steph, have you never tried to find out who your parents were? It seems to me a children's home as good as you say that one was would have made some attempt to identify you."

"I was very young when I left it, Mac, and just a baby when I was left there." Her eyes widened on a thought. "I suppose it does matter that my parents may have been bad — bad blood."

"Steph, for God's sake! What kind of talk is that?" He jerked at the wheel,

249

bouncing the car to a stop at the side of the road. "Look, you," he said in anger, "I know who you are! You're my girl, and that's all that matters! You are, aren't you?"

"Oh, Mac."

"Don't 'Oh Mac' me. I love you, Steph. Get that through your head, and get that chin of yours up. You're a fighter, Steph. You're not going to let anything lick you at this late date, are you?"

"I'm still sort of dazed by it all, Mac. I can't believe it is happening. You, I mean, saying you love me. Oh, are you sure? You're so decent, good! You helped Liz when she was down and now you're helping me . . ."

"Big difference, there, my girl. I love Liz like a big brother should, but you, well, you always did bother the hell out of me . . . " He grinned at her, then slowly sobered. "You're tired, Steph. I'm going to take you home. I probably should have had Dr. Craig take a look at you."

250

"No, no, I'm fine. Mac, what did you tell the doctor?"

"Nothing much. He's an old friend of the family. Your name was not mentioned."

"My name." She stared out into the night, and now she was remembering his mother and the house on Nob Hill. "Mac," she said, not looking at him, "I can't help it that I do not know who I am — who my parents were — but I should not like to deceive anyone anymore. Your mother, your sister, your friends, what about them?"

"Well, what about them? Don't tell me you're a snob at heart, honey. And, if it's a name you're fretting about, how does Mrs. Alexander Dumas MacArthur sound?"

She made a small sound that was not quite laughter, but Mac felt encouraged, and when she asked, "Is that really your name?" he laughed.

"Ask my mother, if you don't believe me," he said, and saw her lips twitch as she almost smiled. "Steph, darling,

I know you must be about exhausted." He took hold of her shoulders, turning her. "I'd like to take you home to the Queen Mother," he told her. "You can't stay in your apartment tonight."

"I can stay with Liz." For a moment, Stephanie frowned into his face. "Mac, I told Liz everything I've told you, but she knew about me. I asked her how she knew, but . . . "

He told her what he knew of the night's beginnings, and added, "I think Glen is suffering right now, Steph. He must feel responsible for what happened."

"Poor Glen. Poor Liz. But I don't want Glen to feel guilty. If I'd told the truth in the beginning . . . " She sighed softly. "But I couldn't. I was too ashamed, and I had my own guilts. Mac, is it true that you love me? I love you, but I'd not want it to be pity you feel."

"But I do feel pity, pity for all you went through alone. I wish I could wipe it completely out of your mind. Sure, I feel pity. I think it's a pity there isn't more joy in the world and that people get themselves so damned mixed up." He gave her shoulders a shake. "But, my girl, if you think for a second that I want to marry you out of pity, you're not in your right mind. At that, maybe you're not, after tonight," he added more gently.

"Mac — Alex MacArthur," she said tiredly, "you've convinced me. Oh, Mac, I love you so . . ."

When they drove on again, the lines the night had put upon their faces had smoothed considerably. It was still fairly early, which surprised them both. "Hungry?" Mac asked.

"No. Are you?"

"Not really."

"I must look awful. I don't remember what happened to my pocketbook, and the apartment door . . . Gosh, Mac, the landlord will wonder."

"I imagine Liz gave him some cock-and-bull story. I wouldn't worry about anything tonight, sweetheart."

She sighed. "All right. You're the boss."

"That reminds me," he said. "You're fired. I'll give you a month's notice, but you're fired." And for a moment his heart seemed to stand still, for the sound he had been waiting for came, softly, tiredly, but real. Stephanie laughed.

"Mac," she asked presently, "shall I have to see Maude?"

"No. I'll take care of everything. She's all right now, Steph. As Glen said, she's happy, talking and laughing with her little brother. She has him back in her mind." He reached and took her hand.

Tears welled, dried. "I wish they could have forgiven me," she said. "I never meant any of them any harm."

"Try not to think of it, darling. Here we are. Lights are on in Liz's apartment, so I guess she's at home."

Liz was at home and Glen was still with her. Stephanie went to them in turn and kissed them, and Mac said there had been enough talk for one night, and asked if Liz had learned to make a decent cup of coffee yet.

"You'll take instant coffee and like it," he was told, and he heard Stephanie laugh again. She was very pale, yet she looked both happy and sad, young and old. Mac reached a swift and immovable decision.

When she had made herself present-able and had had a cup of coffee, he gave her a stern look. "You, my girl, get yourself whatever you need for the night, then come with me."

"What, again?" demanded Liz.

"I'm taking her to the Queen Mother. She'll never get any sleep with you gabbing all night. Glen, thanks for putting the door back on its hinges and appeasing the landlord. Steph, move, will you? Go get what you need."

"Come on, Steph," Liz said. "I'm damned if I know why you'd want to marry such a bossy old man!"

Mac heard Stephanie laughed tiredly as she went with Liz. Glen looked worried. "Mac, do you think it's okay to let Steph see the place so soon?"

"It won't hurt her, Glen, and I do want her to spend the night at my mother's. I figure one look and she'll be glad to."

Stephanie did not even glance toward the kitchen as she and Liz entered her apartment. She packed an overnight bag while Liz commended Mac's decision.

"And, Steph," she added, "thanks for not hating Glen. He feels so bad."

Stephanie gave her a wan smile. "Liz, please, he mustn't. If he hadn't done what he did, I'd still be walking around with the past haunting me. Now, I can forget."

In tears, Liz hugged her, then said, "Let's get out of here. Oh, Steph, weren't you scared out of your wits?"

She thought about it. "Just at first, I guess, Liz, when I saw Maude in the elevator, then I just went sort of numb. I didn't care much one way or the other."

"Don't say that!" They closed the

splintered door behind them and saw Mac approaching down the hall. "I'm glad about you two," Liz whispered.

Stephanie smiled at the half-worried look on Mac's face. "I'm ready to go," she told him, then laughed softly. "Liz, did you know he fired me?"

Mac's eyes blinked, stung, but he grinned. Already, he thought, her healing is beginning. And it was all he wanted, to hear her laugh . . . to make her happy at last.

Mac had made a call to his mother while Stephanie had been packing. So when Stephanie said as he drove toward Nob Hill, "Oh, Mac, are you sure your mother won't mind?" he just grinned.

"As a matter of fact, she's expecting you, honey. I imagine about now she and Greta are rolling out the red carpet."

"You told her, when?"

"While you were packing."

"Oh. Mac — " She turned slightly to look at him. "Mac, I want to tell her. I don't want her not to know about me."

"Plenty of time for that, dear. She's very happy about us. Tonight you sleep; tomorrow you can talk all you want."

Greta had the front door open, and behind her, Althea MacArthur was waiting.

"Welcome home, Stephanie," she said.

Stephanie clung to Mac's hand, a little blinded by tears, and then she said, a bit foolishly, "I brought my needlepoint."

"Bless you, child, come in, come in. Alex, put her bag in Beth's old room. Greta, now we can have some tea and your little sandwiches." And the little woman held out her hand to take Stephanie's. Her eyes were wet, but her voice steady.

"Stephanie, dear, give this blasted chair a turn, will you?"

Mac, heading for the stairway with Stephanie's bag, paused to look back, and he heaved a sigh of pure relief. His mother had a perfect genius for putting people at ease, thought Steph.

Seated close to the Queen, Stephanie was smiling, although her brown eyes showed a glimmering of tears. She had a curious feeling that all her years had had no other aim but this moment.

"I have so much to tell you," she said.

"All in good time, dear," the little woman said. "All in good time."

6

MACARTHUR laughed her daughter's expres-
Well, my dear, are you
at a loss words for once?"

Beth blew out her breath. "But, Mother, it's incredible. And you don't *know*, after all . . . You actually went through all her belongings?"

"There was no one else to do it. I offered as one of her oldest friends. Dear me, such a sad state of affairs. I always thought there was quite a large trust fund, but apparently not. The old house is mortgaged to the hilt. She was on the point of being evicted, or might have been if it had not been for her name . . . "

Beth, who had been pacing about, sat down close to her mother's wheelchair. "Mama," she said earnestly, "if what you suspect *is* true it will mean that

Steph comes from one of our finest old families."

"Don't be a snob, Beth. Alex doesn't care about such nonsense and neither should you."

"Just the same, the name Cunningham *used* to carry a lot of weight." Beth stood up. "But of course the whole thing is ridiculous. Just because Miss Cunningham's brother-in-law was named Stephen. What was it? Stephen Ward?"

"Yes, and he was a soldier. Madge ran off with him and they could have had a child."

"Mother, you want it so badly you're not using your head."

"Try Alex's number again."

"No. Steph told you last night they were going ring shopping. They'll probably be out half the night."

"Don't be so cross, Beth. I have no intention of telling Stephanie anything until I'm sure. And if I'm wrong, no harm done."

"But you think you're right."

"Stephanie says she will be twenty-five in September. She was eleven months old when she was left at the Home on August fourteenth of that year and September fourteenth became her first birthday. Madge Cunningham Ward left here about twenty-six years ago . . ."

Beth picked up the old family album. "I have to admit to the resemblance, Mother, although Madge looks much older than Steph is now."

"You didn't see Stephanie when she wore her hair long like Madge's in that picture. Stephanie looked older than her years."

Beth set the album aside to rifle through faded papers in a cardboard box. "Miss Cunningham was certainly careful to keep Madge's letters and mementos intact for someone so bitter about her marrying."

"Alicia Cunningham was a born spinster, Beth. She had her father to look after for years *and* Madge, and to my knowledge she never had a beau or wanted one."

"How much older than Madge was she?"

"Fifteen or sixteen years."

Beth pushed the box aside and reseated herself. "Well, I hope you're right, Mama, but you're going to have a tough time proving it."

"There are agencies to do tracing, and Alex is resourceful. The mere fact that Stephen Ward was a soldier should make him easy to find, if he's alive, which I doubt."

"How so?"

"It wouldn't make sense for him to be alive, or Madge, either. One or the other abandoned that baby, and I think it was the father, which would mean his wife had died."

Beth rolled her eyes. "You read too many whodunits. Well, I better get along home. I must say, I never thought my little brother would go so head over heels."

"Beth, you do like Stephanie, don't you?"

"Yes, and I'm surprised. Well, ta-ta for now, Mother. I hope you won't be too disappointed when you're proved wrong."

"Goodbye, dear. Oh, there you are, Greta! Did Alex say whether he and Stephanie would be by this evening?"

"You know he didn't, Thea, but if they find the right ring I imagine they will be."

"I'll want to talk to Alex alone, so you take Stephanie off on some pretext."

Greta laughed. "Even if it turns out you are wrong, you've had a lovely time over it. And, if you are right, Thea, Stephanie may feel very unhappy not to have known Miss Cunningham before she died."

"Perhaps it's better this way, Greta. Miss Cunningham was a stubborn old fool. Stephanie might not appreciate the way she treated Madge, just disowning her."

The telephone rang and Greta answered it, then relayed the message:

Alex and Stephanie would be by for a while that evening to show off Stephanie's engagement ring.

"Good. Greta, you are a treasure."

"Glad you realize it. When they get here, Thea, leave it to me. I'll take Stephanie upstairs and show her the quilt I'm making. I've been wondering what I'd do with it when it's finished. Do you think Stephanie would like to have it?"

"She'll love it. Greta, you do think I'm right, don't you?"

Much as Beth had done, Greta rolled her eyes. "I hope so, for your sake, Thea. I'm sure I couldn't care less who Stephanie's parents were, and I doubt if she does now."

Stephanie was so busy she had no time to dwell upon the past.

There had been Liz's wedding, and then helping the newlyweds get settled in their apartment when they returned from a week's honeymoon. Plus her own upcoming wedding, and the business of breaking in her replacement. Then, one night nearly a month after Maude Nelson had tried to kill her, Stephanie learned, at last, who she was.

She listened, quiet, dry-eyed, her hand in Mac's gone cold, but she managed a smile for the little woman who spoke so gently, softening the part about Miss Cunningham, who could not defend herself.

"None of it seems real," she said at last, "but I'm grateful to you all. Grateful, chiefly, because I know you did it for my sake." She bent and kissed Mac's mother. "And because I know you'd not have changed toward me had I been proved the illegitimate daughter of some poor wayward girl."

"For that I thank you, dear," Althea said.

"And now that's out of the way," Mac said, "you can forget it, Steph. Stephanie MacArthur suits you better than any other name and I wish to the devil you'd hurry up and take it."

"Just two weeks to go and a million

266

things to do beforehand. Thank heaven for Beth's help." Stephanie laughed suddenly. "How odd," she said, "to know who I am at last and find it nice to know, but unreal. I never knew any of them." Her dark eyes moved from Mac's mother to Greta to Mac and back. "You are real," she said earnestly, "and all the family I need."

"For God's sake, Steph, don't be so dramatic," Mac half shouted. "And let's get out of here! I need a drink. You're the damndest orphan I ever knew."

"Oh shut up, Mac," Stephanie said, and the two women, close to tears, suddenly laughed, and the drama of the hour was relegated to its proper place.

17

"I'M going to miss you around here," Liz said.

"I'm going to miss working, in a way, but I can hardly wait to start furnishing our house. I really could skip the honeymoon abroad." Stephanie smiled, then shrugged. "But don't tell Mac that, Liz. He's dying to show me all the cathedrals and mausoleums and whatever he wished he had designed, and it will be thrilling. I'd just be satisfied with a lot less."

"Mac wants to give you the world, Steph. Don't knock it."

They were in the coffee shop drinking Cokes and taking a rather long break, but it was Friday afternoon and Stephanie's last day of work.

"What's the big idea? Do you two know how long you've been down here gabbing your heads off while the business goes to pot?" They swung about to find Mac standing near, scowling fiercely.

"Don't look at me," Stephanie said airily. "I don't work here anymore."

Liz laughed. She watched as Mac seated himself and took Stephanie's hand. He groaned. "I tell you, Liz," he said. "I view my future with alarm. She gets harder to handle every day."

Liz stood. "I leave you two lovebirds at this point," she said grandly. "You look as if you are in pretty good hands, Mac, and I know when three is a crowd. See you tonight, Steph."

"Hey," Mac said as Liz walked away. He turned to Stephanie. "What did she mean, see you tonight?"

"Beth's coming over with more instructions for us and to get last-minute wedding announcements addressed."

He shook his head. "All this fuss. I've a good mind to leave you waiting at the church."

"What's the matter, darling? Have I been neglecting you?"

"You certainly have."

"Well, Beth won't be over before eight and it's just three-thirty now. What do you say we play hookey?"

"Now that's more like it. Maybe I won't leave you waiting at the church after all."

Stephanie laughed and tucked her hand around his arm as they left the coffee shop.

"Happy, Mac?" she asked, pausing a moment on the busy sunlit street to look up at him.

"Not as happy as I expect to be soon."

"I know. I'm so happy I'd elope with you right this minute, if you'd like, and forget the big wedding."

"What? And break Beth's heart?" he mocked. "Come on, girl, don't just stand there. Let's go down to Fisherman's Wharf and have some crab Louie, and then I'll drown you."

"Whatever makes you happy, love."

He grinned. She was healing fast, the future looked bright, and it was a beautiful summer day.

WITH SOMEBODY ELSE
Theresa Charles

Rosamond sets off for Cornwall with Hugo to meet his family, blissfully unaware of the shocks in store for her.

A SUMMER FOR STRANGERS
Claire Hamilton

Because she had lost her job, her flat and she had no money, Tabitha agreed to pose as Adam's future wife although she believed the scheme to be deceitful and cruel.

VILLA OF SINGING WATER
Angela Petron

The disquieting incidents that occurred at the Vatican and the Colosseum did not trouble Jan at first, but then they became increasingly unpleasant and alarming.

DOCTOR NAPIER'S NURSE
Pauline Ash

When cousins Midge and Derry are entered as probationer nurses on the same day but at different hospitals they agree to exchange identities.

A GIRL LIKE JULIE
Louise Ellis

Caroline absolutely adored Hugh Barrington, but then Julie Crane came into their lives. Julie was the kind of girl who attracts men without even trying.

COUNTRY DOCTOR
Paula Lindsay

When Evan Richmond bought a practice in a remote country village he did not realise that a casual encounter would lead to the loss of his heart.

ENCORE
Helga Moray

Craig and Janet realise that their true happiness lies with each other, but it is only under traumatic circumstances that they can be reunited.

NICOLETTE
Ivy Preston

When Grant Alston came back into her life, Nicolette was faced with a dilemma. Should she follow the path of duty or the path of love?

THE GOLDEN PUMA
Margaret Way

Catherine's time was spent looking after her father's Queensland farm. But what life was there without David, who wasn't interested in her?

HOSPITAL BY THE LAKE
Anne Durham

Nurse Marguerite Ingleby was always ready to become personally involved with her patients, to the despair of Brian Field, the Senior Surgical Registrar, who loved her.

VALLEY OF CONFLICT
David Farrell

Isolated in a hostel in the French Alps, Ann Russell sees her fiancé being seduced by a young girl. Then comes the avalanche that imperils their lives.

NURSE'S CHOICE
Peggy Gaddis

A proposal of marriage from the incredibly handsome and wealthy Reagan was enough to upset any girl — and Brooke Martin was no exception.

A DANGEROUS MAN
Anne Goring

Photographer Polly Burton was on safari in Mombasa when she met enigmatic Leon Hammond. But unpredictability was the name of the game where Leon was concerned.

PRECIOUS INHERITANCE
Joan Moules

Karen's new life working for an authoress took her from Sussex to a foreign airstrip and a kidnapping; to a real life adventure as gripping as any in the books she typed.

VISION OF LOVE
Grace Richmond

When Kathy takes over the rundown country kennels she finds Alec Stinton, a local vet, very helpful. But their friendship arouses bitter jealousy and a tragedy seems inevitable.

CRUSADING NURSE
Jane Converse

It was handsome Dr. Corbett who opened Nurse Susan Leighton's eyes and who set her off on a lonely crusade against some powerful enemies and a shattering struggle against the man she loved.

WILD ENCHANTMENT
Christina Green

Rowan's agreeable new boss had a dream of creating a famous perfume using her precious Silverstar, but Rowan's plans were very different.

DESERT ROMANCE
Irene Ord

Sally agrees to take her sister Pam's place as La Chartreuse the dancer, but she finds out there is more to it than dyeing her hair red and looking like her sister.

HEART OF ICE
Marie Sidney

How was January to know that not only would the warmth of the Swiss people thaw out her frozen heart, but that she too would play her part in helping someone to live again?

LUCKY IN LOVE
Margaret Wood

Companion-secretary to wealthy gambler Laura Duxford, who lived in Monaco, seemed to Melanie a fabulous job. Especially as Melanie had already lost her heart to Laura's son, Julian.

NURSE TO PRINCESS JASMINE
Lilian Woodward

Nick's surgeon brother, Tom, performs an operation on an Arabian princess, and she invites Tom, Nick and his fiancé to Omander, where a web of deceit and intrigue closes about them.

THE WAYWARD HEART
Eileen Barry

Disaster-prone Katherine's nickname was "Kate Calamity", but her boss went too far with an outrageous proposal, which because of her latest disaster, she could not refuse.

FOUR WEEKS IN WINTER
Jane Donnelly

Tessa wasn't looking forward to meeting Paul Mellor again — she had made a fool of herself over him once before. But was Orme Jared's solution to her problem likely to be the right one?

SURGERY BY THE SEA
Sheila Douglas

Medical student Meg hadn't really wanted to go and work with a G.P. on the Welsh coast although the job had its compensations. But Owen Roberts was certainly not one of them!

HEAVEN IS HIGH
Anne Hampson

The new heir to the Manor of Marbeck had been found. But it was rather unfortunate that when he arrived unexpectedly he found an uninvited guest, complete with stetson and high boots.

LOVE WILL COME
Sarah Devon

June Baker's boss was not really her idea of her ideal man, but when she went from third typist to boss's secretary overnight she began to change her mind.

ESCAPE TO ROMANCE
Kay Winchester

Oliver and Jean first met on Swale Island. They were both trying to begin their lives afresh, but neither had bargained for complications from the past.